S Stois

DANIEL WOODRELL

Daniel Woodrell was born in the Missouri Ozarks, where he still lives. He left school and enlisted in the Marines the week he turned seventeen, and received his BA at the age of twenty-seven. He also has an MFA from the Iowa Writers' Workshop. He is the author of eight novels including *Winter's Bone*, the film of which was nominated for four Oscars in 2011, *Woe to Live On*, the basis for the film *Ride with the Devil* directed by Ang Lee, and *Tomato Red*, which won the PEN West Award for fiction in 1999. Five of his novels have been selected as *New York Times* Notable Books of the year. This is his first collection of stories.

* * *

'Gripping ... As with Woodrell's highly praised novel *Winter's Bone*, the Ozarks provide a dark, almost fairytale-like setting for a population of scarred and hood-eyed loners lost in pain, drugs and memory... Woodrell whittles his stories into shape with a serrated knife, and while the language of his characters is a constant surprise with those oblique turns-of-phrase – "Her britches are pale and slicked onto her booty like they started as steam puffs" – the curious sideways progression of his plots is what I find most enrapturing. All the stories carry in them not so much a twist in the tale as a final, fatal jerk upward of the knife, a killing blow that punctures the lungs and compels the reader to let out a stunned last gasp of breath.'
George Pendle, *Financial Times*

'Short, sharp and expertly crafted, these stories contain more pertinent comment on the human condition than a hundred more self-consciously "literary" collections'
Big Issue

'Woodrell engages with these lives in a way that transcends the stereotypes of rural America, investing caricatured figures with human interest. In a tight navigation of narrative voice, Woodrell manages to turn candid detachment into a form of rough poetic truth, even though the lives of his characters remain far removed from the world of literary sentiment.'
Ivan Juritz, *Times Literary Supplement*

'A writer whose words flow with the elemental power of Cormac McCarthy, William Gay, and Chris Offutt, he's chipped an impression of the Ozarks and its people in stone that will endure time ... Let these stories be your Bible.'
Chris Talbott, *Associated Press*

'Woodrell's prose is spare, even stern, yet capable of unexpected lyricism. Amid the rage, despair, and hatred his characters live with, he teases out and diplays their deep stores of love and loyalty, and a surprisingly bracing humor.'
Kate Tuttle, *Boston Globe*

'The first and most important task of any piece of writing is to draw the reader in, to engage them and compel them to keep going. On that count, and on pretty much every other one, Woodrell succeeds. *The Outlaw Album* shows his complete mastery of voice, tone, language, and pacing ... an amazing collection.'
Jeff Baker, *Oregonian*

'The human desperation behind the violence is gripping. If anyone understands what motivates a man to keep shooting a corpse with a squirrel rifle, it's Woodrell.'
Melissa Maerz, *Entertainment Weekly*

'Riveting, enigmatic, lyrically blood-soaked with darkness, violence and revenge, but above all these things it is Mr. Woodrell's sparse and disturbing to-the-bone prose that mesmerizes us.'
Sam Millar, *New York Journal of Books*

'He has moved beyond the noir of his earlier work into something that encompasses a greater spectrum of understanding. He has cemented his role as one of America's greatest writers.' William Hastings, *Industrial Worker Book Review*

Daniel Woodrell

THE OUTLAW ALBUM

Stories

SCEPTRE

First published in Great Britain in 2011 by Sceptre
An imprint of Hodder & Stoughton
An Hachette UK company

First published in paperback in 2012

1

A CIP catalogue record for this title is available from the British Library

ISBN 9781444735789

Printed and bound by Clays Ltd, St Ives plc

Hodder & Stoughton policy is to use papers that are natural, renewable and
recyclable products and made from wood grown in sustainable forests. The logging
and manufacturing processes are expected to conform to the environmental
regulations of the country of origin.

Hodder & Stoughton Ltd
338 Euston Road
London NW1 3BH

www.sceptrebooks.com

And I am learning not to separate these beings
charged with violence from the sky
in which their desires revolve.
—Albert Camus, "Summer in Algiers"

Contents

The Echo of
Neighborly Bones

Once Boshell finally killed his neighbor he couldn't seem to quit killing him. He killed him again whenever he felt unloved or blue or simply had empty hours facing him. The first time he killed the man, Jepperson, an opinionated foreigner from Minnesota, he kept to simple Ozark tradition and used a squirrel rifle, bullet to the heart, classic and effective, though there were spasms of the limbs and even a lunge of big old Jepperson's body that seemed like he was about to take a step, flee, but he died in stride and collapsed against a fence post. Boshell took the body to the woods on his deer scooter and piled heavy rocks on the man, trying to keep nature back from the flesh, the parts of nature that have teeth or beaks.

For most of a week Boshell was content with killing his neighbor just once, then came a wet spattering Sunday, the dish went out and he couldn't see the ball game on TV, so he snuck away to the pile and cleared the rocks from the head and chest. Jepperson had died with a sort of sneer on his face, thick lips crooked to the side, his dead eyes yet looking down his nose in calm contempt. That look and Jepperson's frequent sharp comments had months ago prompted Boshell to put a sticker on his truck bumper that read, "I Don't Give a Damn HOW You Did It Up North!" Even dead, the man goaded a fella. The falling wet slicked his hair back from his greening face, and his lips seemed to move under the drops, flutter, like he had still another insult he was about to let fly. Boshell hunted a stout stick and thumped the corpse. Thumped the stick enough times to snuff a live man, thumped enough to feel better about the rain and the washed-out ball game, then went home to his wife, Evelyn.

She said, "Wherever'd you get off to?"

"Oh, you know. I just can't get to feelin' done with the son of a bitch."

"In all this rain?"

"I'm gonna have to move him. He's goin' high now the cold snap broke. Someplace further from the fire road."

"Well, his wife's got herself some company today over there, and they been sniffin' about, lookin' places." She

4

pointed across the creek where there was a big metal barn, four penned horses, and a mess of guineas running loose, pecking and gabbling. Four people in raincoats and sagging hats stood near the horses, with their boots on the bottom fence rail and their elbows on the top. "Best wait 'til they leave."

"I'll try."

Only two days later Boshell checked the can for morning coffee and found it empty, so he went out to kill the man again, kill himself awake without any joe to drink. Bird droppings had spotted the rocks over the man, and one of the hands had moved somehow so that a pinky stuck from between the rocks. The little bit of the pinky that showed had been chewed at, nibbled, torn. Boshell pulled the rocks away until Jepperson was open to the October sky. He went back to his truck for a hatchet, a beat-up hatchet with a dinged, uneven blade and a cracked handle. He stood over the corpse and said, "Say it. Go on and say it, why don't you?" Then he sank the hatchet into the chest area and stood back to admire the way the handle stood up straight from the wound. The handle was directly below Jepperson's nose, and his eyes appeared to find it to be kind of funny business, having a hatchet in his chest.

"Glad you like it."

Boshell left the blade in the man's chest, then dragged the corpse to his truck. He tossed a tarp over the raised handle and all, but knew he wouldn't likely run into anybody, not where he was going. He steered the truck downhill going west, onto a creek bed with shallow puddles but no flow, and eased south over the pale and reddish rocks, the truck bucking during the rougher patches. He turned uphill below the old home place, the land now overgrown by brambles and deserted by residents, and parked on the slope. One wall of a house with an askew window could be seen still standing back in the thicket. Boshell's people had lived on this dirt until the government annexed it for the National Forest in the 1950s, and lazy old time had slowly reclaimed the place for trees and weeds and possums. He came here often, to sit and wonder, and feel robbed of all these acres.

He shoved the corpse from the truck bed, and the hatchet fell loose when the body thumped to ground. Boshell set the blade back into the wound, then tamped it in snug with a boot stomp. The hatchet fell free twice more before he got Jepperson up to where his grandma's garden had been laid and she'd grown the tangiest okra he'd ever had and oddly shaped but sweet tomatoes you just couldn't find anymore. The corpse nodded when dragged and the head bent a bit to the side, as if he was taking an interest in this trip, noting the details, setting the picture in his mind.

Boshell said, "This all was ours, ours up until foreigners like you'n yours got here from up north with fancy notions'n bank money and *improved* everything for us."

He looked on Jepperson, with his face yet smug in death, and remembered when the dead man said in that voice that came from way high in the nose, "If I come across one more eaten guinea, I'll shoot your dog." And Boshell had said, "That ain't the neighborly way, mister. If'n Bitsy was to rip a guinea or two, just tell us." And the dead man, so much younger and bigger and flush with money and newcomer attitudes, said, "I don't give two shits about being neighborly with you people. Have you not noticed that?"

Now Boshell nudged the corpse with a boot, put his toe to the chin, and shoved the head until the face was up again. He started to crouch, but the scent was too high, and he stood back a step to say, "They go for about a dollar fifty a bird, neighbor—still seem worth it?"

The old, original well was sided by short, stacked walls of stones. The well had gone dry long ago, in Grandpa's time, before the coughing killed him, and a slab rock the color of dirt had been slid over the gap so no playing child or adult drinking shine in the dark would wander over and fall into the hole, bust a leg or a neck. The hole was but eight feet deep, and there were a few shards of glass and earthenware scattered about the bottom where the spout had sealed shut after the water table dropped.

"Your new home, neighbor. Maybe I'll be back to tell you about this place. Family history."

Evelyn made his favorite dish that night. She'd thawed a couple of quail, split them and fried them in the black skillet, served them with sides of chow-chow and bean salad. Boshell had whiskey, she had her daily glass of beer, and they watched the evening news on an East Coast channel the satellite dish pulled into their front room. The traffic reports made them laugh, shake their heads, and the weather was interesting to watch, what with the cold northern temperatures and early snowflakes swirling down between sun-thwarting buildings into gray canyons, but of no use. When a segment about lost dogs in Brooklyn came on he tried to turn the TV off, but Evelyn was bawling before he could find the button.

She ran outside and Boshell followed. She rushed past the ranks of firewood, the chopping block, a wheelless Nova that would never be fixed, and sagged against an oak tree lightning had split. Bitsy had crawled home hurt and collapsed beneath the split tree, gutshot, vomiting, looking up at Ev with baffled, resigned eyes, and it took two hours for her to bleed out and die with a last windy sound and a little flutter. Strands of silver hair waved across Evelyn's face, and her hands clenched onto her dress and squeezed the wad of cloth. The horses across the creek neighed in their pen, and the big house beyond was dark.

"Oh, Ev," he said. "We'll soon get you another."

"There wasn't never but the one Bitsy. Just the one."

Later, when the moon had settled, Boshell slid from bed and dressed. He fetched a big flashlight and went out back to the toolshed. He shoved cobwebs in the corner aside and searched among hoes, rakes, a busted scythe, until he came across his old three-tined frog gig. He tapped the ground with the gig as he walked, and started down the dry creek bed, splashing light over all those rocks, whistling like a child.

Uncle

A cradle won't hold my baby. My baby is two hundred pounds in a wheelchair and hard to push uphill but silent all the time. He can't talk since his head got hurt, which I did to him. I broke into his head with a mattocks and he hasn't said a thing to me nor nobody else since. Uncle is Ma's evil brother and there never was a day when I wasn't afraid of him, even when he gave me striped candy from his pocket or let me drive the tractor in the yard.

Before Uncle became my baby, when he was a man, myself and Ma both tried to never be alone inside with him, tried to never even stand too close outside, as he was born with a pair of devils in his chest and the one just eggs on the other and neither ever rests, and last fall he seen my undies on the clothesline moving in the wind and said to me kind of joyful and mean, Old enough to bleed, old enough to breed.

I was waiting on him ever since, the slide-in move under my quilt as I slept, the whiskery rub on my cheek, the fingers riding roughshod over my skin like cowboys hunting an Indian to blame. Ma always was scared to chase him off, or even let on she noticed the things he done.

The day I come across the mattocks in the shadows and swung down on his head and rendered him into my own big quiet baby, there was a girl. The girl was yelling high-pitched the way they did, out there in the old barn where Uncle took them. The barn sets near where the house was once, long ago, a good ways down the cow pasture from where the house is now, and the wood hangs at a tilt on the sides of the barn, all dried up and flaky from sun and rain and freeze since Ma's ma was younger than me, and the roof has fallen open in a bunch of spots, but there's some hay put by inside, pitched around loose, and a shock of old garden tools leaned in the corner, and small birds black as pepper come and go from the slanted rafters. This one screamed louder than most, and screamed loudest in between sentences she said, such as, There's no need for this! Get off of me! Stop! Stop! Please, stop!

Uncle culled these girls from down on the river, which they come here for, and flows just yonder over our ridge and down a steep hill. They come here from where there are crowds of people bunched in tight to loll along our crystal water in college shirts and bikinis, smoking weed and drinking too much, laughing all the way while their canoes spin on the river like bugs twirling in a spider's web. Mostly they don't know what they're doing, but the river is not too raging or anything. Everybody thinks they can do that river when they stand looking at it up at Heaney Cross, where they rent the canoes and the water is smooth. Uncle dicks them when he catches them, on the smelly damp hay in the old barn with the open spots above leaking light on his big behind bouncing white and glary on some girl whose eyes won't blink anymore. But this yelling girl was giving him a tussle, clawing at him and such as that, scratching him under his eyes so blood laid a narrow path down his face and dropped from his chin onto her chest and bare boobies, and Uncle dicked her even harder in his own blood. She had brown hair that was bright blond on top in perfect streaks, which looked pretty and special, something I might ought to try, and stopped yelling because he had his hands on her throat.

Uncle stood once his own breaths slowed, stood and hooked his bibs up and left her lay there, and then is when I slunk into the barn and knelt.

Let's get you out of here, lady. Sometimes he comes back.

I hauled her up and made her move, trying to get her to the spring pooled under our ridge where her canoe would likely be waiting. Uncle looked for loners, mostly, and understood that the law here ain't eager to come into our woods after him, so he was bold as an idiot sometimes, when he smoked powder or drunk a bunch. I held hands with her down the trail, which switches back and forth and is steep, with little rocks slippery underfoot, and she didn't say a word. Get in the spring, I said, and when she didn't, I pushed her. The cold water shocked her face into a different cast, brought color to her skin. The water in the pool shimmered like glass, and you could see the polish on your toenails standing in there. I made a shallow cup of my hands and sloshed what water I could onto her skin, which had tanned, and she wore earrings I liked, the kind that hung low from the ears but didn't flop around all spaz every time your head moved, with purple glass in the low part, my favorite color. Her body had got to be one big goose bump, plump and trembling, her lips pressed together and mumbly.

There was a bird book in her canoe that put a name to all of them it looked like, with inked pictures. I said, Come on, lady, get the hell away from here. And, listen, if you run to the law, well, he'll know, and pretty quick he'll know where you live, too. You won't want that. Nobody wants that. She got into the canoe, and I gave it a strong shove out to the main current and waved goodbye. She didn't raise a paddle, even, until she was near gone from sight.

Back in the pasture, he said to me, She leave anything good?

Didn't she have on a necklace? I said. Seems like there was a skinny golden one around her neck before she laid down on the hay. Must be it flew off or broke loose.

You might be right, he said, and headed for the barn. I think maybe you are. He started staring at the messed straw and dirt and bird puddles on the ground. Golden, was it?

I said, Just there, I think. She laid just there. Then I eased to the dark nearby corner and let my hand drop to the mattocks handle. Maybe you could find it best with your fingers, feel for it. He got on his knees to feel the dirt for gold, and I hoisted that mattocks overhead and slammed down like I was busting the cow pond ice open in winter, so the whole herd could drink.

There was a good deal of blood, and his arms and legs and fingers and all shook pretty jittery for a spell. His face was to the hay and the blood built a creek down his backbone. He messed himself so I could smell it strong standing back from him a distance.

I had sat down and started poking him with a stick by the time Ma got home from work. He wasn't shaking that much anymore. She screamed, yanked on her hair, called for an ambulance, and asked me, Who did this? I said, The last girl he was after done it. Ma said, Oh, my, if he don't die what'll we do?

Ma works, so he became my baby to take care of once they turned him out of the hospital. He was there almost all summer, s'posed to pass away any ol' day but he never. Doctor said, He'll need constant care, like a new-born. Ma said, I got a job already—he's yours, hon.

You finally get an ogre under your thumb and you can't hardly keep from torturing him some at first. That's how it started with my baby, torturing him a little bit now and then, but his face hardly twitched and his eyes just stayed focused on something over yon behind the clouds that he couldn't look away from, so it wasn't as much fun as you figure torturing an ogre should be. I wheeled him out to the yard in thunderstorms and left him set there in his metal chair. Rain beat on him and blown leaves stuck to his face, but he never caught pneumonia or a lightning bolt. I poured bird feed into a bread pan and set him along the tree line with the pan on his lap. One day I put him in a frilly pink dress Ma had and did his hair up in a French bun and used the whole bucket of Ma's makeup on him—eyeliner, rouge, lipstick—and wheeled him out front to the road and left him sit all day beside the mailbox, for every passing neighbor and stranger to see, until Ma found him and wheeled him back to the house. Then she and me spent the evening curling his hair like Shirley Temple and laughing, hooking bras on him, drawing movie star moles on his cheeks, searching for just the right spot until he looked like a disease had got him, trying all the shades of lipstick on his sagged mouth, and cherry red worked best, we figured, with his complexion.

I had to feed him pabulum with a cereal spoon and

squirt water into his throat so his pills would go down. He could chew, which must be the last reflex to shut off in a body, or something. Once I rolled him all the way around on the paved road to the river, and shoved him into the water up to his neck. He made a picture, with only his head poked up for turtles to rest on, while tiny white waves lapped at his jowls, and the chair scooted slightly in the current. I left him there for fate to find him easy, and floated away to the bridge, where I dove and dove for tourist treasure that might've washed down from all the canoes that take spills upstream, and let the sun dry me after, then dawdled back to where he waited. He wasn't exactly where I left him, but was fine, cold but fine, and I had a terrible awful time wheeling such a big fat wet baby uphill to home.

Twice a day I slid the thunder pan under him and wiped his butt, and every three days I shaved his face with an old straight razor in case my hands shook and he got cut to ribbons by accident. I wiped the drool from his chin when he slobbered, which was always, spent most of my time with him, and in about a month I caught myself singing at him, "You are my sunshine . . ." and such—baby music, the kind you coo more than sing. I puked out the front door, catching myself that way, the first time. It was awful, awful, singing happy words to a baby that had done so much bad in this world, but soon it started to happen again, about every day, and I got used to catching myself singing to him, accepted it as a human thing of mystery.

He was helpless, and I took to wondering if Uncle was still evil now that he'd become a helpless baby. Do babies learn evil in the run of their days, or bring it with them from the other side of all that you can see? He drooled and I held a rag to his lips, and wheeled him outside into the fresh air and bright light, shoved him along the driveway, to and fro, singing.

It was coming up on Halloween when I first caught my baby's eyes following me across the room. Then it got to where every time I spun around quick, his eyes were on me, and not on my face, neither. Uncle was yet alive inside that big old baby, and his eyes was wanting what babies don't even know about. When he raised a hand to swat a fly, I peed down my legs and ran around inside the house bumping every wall. Come morning I shoved him to the paved road and around to the hill and down to the bridge. The air hung gray and cool and I could see fish in the water, still in the flow with their noses pointed upstream. I wheeled Uncle to the far edge of the bridge, where a drunk in a truck had torn away the railing, and pushed him to the edge. I dabbed the slobber rag to his mouth, then looked into his eyes and saw how babies do change so fast. I tossed the slobber rag into the river and it made a small shadow over the fish before the current whisked it past. I'd been making him well; now I needed to make him right.

My baby ain't meant for this world.

Twin Forks

Morrow wondered if he might soon die because of a beautiful girl from his teens he'd never had the nerve to approach. This thought preoccupied him as he collected fees from campers at dusk and watched shadows on the hillsides for odd patterns, shifty movements, studied parked cars he wasn't sure he recognized, or looked into new faces for any intimation of treachery. He walked about quickly but fought the urge to assume a crouch when crossing open spaces. He was most concerned about ambush when he collected coins from the campground laundry and had his back to the door, or helped beach a canoe that arrived as the gloaming settled. Sometimes he made himself a target at twilight on the riverbank while looking downstream toward Spawt Mill, where in a single summery moment she became fixed in his desires as the perfection of skin and laughter he would always yearn for, but on that day overwhelmed his senses, left him wordless and ashamed.

The sheriff had said, "You probably should've shot him while you could do it legal and get it over with. He might be back for you, or you might not ever see him again, who knows with meth-heads. But you surely will want to be ready if ever he does come around for you, and that could be at any time from now on." Morrow had two employees, and after five days the younger one, a man named Sky, quit, saying, "I got a bunch of kids, man—I can't take the risk he'll shoot me thinkin' I'm you."

"I understand. Thanks for staying with me as long as you have."

December past, when Morrow was shown the property, the seller had been present on the grounds and having a meltdown. He wore a long, rough overcoat and walked to each campsite with a target pistol in hand, shouting lamentations as he fired farewell bullets at trees and picnic tables. He said, "I guess God don't want me to have this place. I guess God's got other plans for me. I guess..." The pop-pops of the pistol seemed small, muted by the forest and the river, but his words were loud and his confusion painful to hear. Morrow winced whenever the man spoke. The realtor, Nan Colvin, a young countrywoman with ruddled mud on her boots and a no-fuss hairstyle, said, "I'm sorry. You shouldn't be seeing this." She took Morrow's arm and walked him away from the store, onto the one-lane bridge abutting the property. They stood near the center, leaning on the heavy iron railing to admire the river, a river fed by springs and running clear and cold, fifty-six degrees year-round. The seller had wandered farther, past the canoe racks and beyond sight, but was still shooting, shouting, possibly weeping. "He's such a good churchgoing man, you know, that he wouldn't sell beer, not at all. Not a can, not a bottle. Nor cigarettes. It's a real principled stand to take, I guess, somethin' folks ought to admire, but beer is about forty percent of sales on the river. He's broke now."

"Things happen for a reason."

"You think?"

"I used to come here as a kid."

"Is that so? Must've been extra wonderful back then, I bet, huh?"

Morrow was down from Nebraska, escaping fresh memories by chasing after old ones, looking for something that might spark his blood awake, make it hop lively in his veins again. Nan had read his e-mails with care and selected this property for him, and he liked everything about the place—the steep hillsides of forest stripped for winter, the dour gray rock bluffs crouched near the river, the lonesome mumble of the passing wind, and these untamed people who shot at things to so plainly announce their sorrow.

She said, "I know this seems kind of wild out here."

"That's what I always liked about it."

"He'll listen to any offer."

Morrow made a lowball offer before supper that day, an offer that could seem insulting to both Nan and the seller, but a few weeks later the offer was accepted. He arrived at the Twin Forks Store and Campground in early March, driving a pickup truck with everything he expected to need stacked neatly in the bed. He intended to change his habits in new surroundings, give his system a shake, so he arrived without many of his once-favorite things: the antique liquor cabinet with the copper top his father had left to him, a box stacked with discs of music that had once made his feet move in ecstasy but that he didn't expect to listen to again. He'd taken all of his golfing trophies down from shelves in the den and tossed them into a trash can at the curb, then returned to drop four pair of handmade shoes and his wristwatch on top of the trophies. That same night he drove to downtown Omaha and placed a set of customized golf clubs on a sidewalk near the bus station and drove away with a raised hand blocking the rearview mirror so he couldn't look back. He did keep a stuffed buffalo head he'd bought on impulse at a garage sale in Lincoln, because the eyes seemed to know him, his pump shotgun for hunting game birds, one box of favorite books. Several pictures of his daughters were saved and brought along, but none of their mother.

By late May he had acquired a routine suited to this new version of himself: wake above the store before dawn, walk to the river, hang his robe on a low limb, plunge in and swim upstream until his arms balked, then float back to his robe as first light began to raise the sky. There would be coffee boiling over freshened campfires, bacon sizzling, trout split and dropped into the grease, and as he passed the earliest to rise he'd wave and they'd wave back. He'd open the store early, skin numbed by the river and feeling tightened ten years younger, the smell of the outdoors drying into his hair.

He hired two relatives of Nan's to wrangle canoes and help out in general, a blood uncle named Royce, and Sky, who he took to be a ceremonial uncle of some sort, while he tended to the store. The locals who came in were often people of a kind he hadn't truly believed still existed but found rewarding to meet: pioneer-lean old men who poached deer whenever hungry and wouldn't pay taxes, their wives wearing gray braids and cowboy hats, clasp knives sheathed at their belts; men with the beards of prophets who read the Bible at a certain slant and could build anything, their women smelling of lavender, in gingham and work boots; folks living hidden in the hills and only reluctantly coming into contact with the conventional world for want of baby formula or headache powders. A few of these customers lingered to chat, but most said all they had to say with a slow nod hello and a jerk of the chin on the way out. There were some he didn't want to linger, squint-faced men with cursive tattoos garbled in shades of blue, who cleaned his shelves of Sudafed and red matchsticks, then returned in a few days hoping to buy more of the same. Royce, who seemed slow in offering helpful advice to an outsider, finally said, "Mr. Morrow, them fellas is buyin' all that so they can drive over the hill there and hide somewhere to cook up drugs. The red part from the matches and grains from them pills both help make the recipe."

"There's so much I don't know."

"That's lesson one."

Campers with children preferred the picnic tables that had been shot, because kids liked rubbing the holes, sticking their fingers inside while imagining exciting events that had led to gunfire erupting on this very spot. Not every table had been shot, and adults wanted to have rights to that exotic detail in any recounting of their vacations, also, and would wait for one to become unoccupied, then rush the family over to claim it, which sometimes caused tensions between the quicker and slower families, a little squabbling, which Morrow usually went out to settle. Come winter he'd fix this problem by blasting every table in the campground, and the various signs nailed to trees, too, but for this season he'd walk among the tents of many sizes and listen, bob his head as he absorbed more or less the same old story, then offer the children of the losing family cold drinks and bags of chips to distract them from whining about bullet holes. Sometimes he watched the children frolic—with skin browning and bug bites lumped on their necks, so many years spread unopened before them—and have a strong sense that he knew the true reason he'd returned here without allowing himself to investigate his memories and make it plain. That changed one day when Sky had traffic court at the county seat, and Morrow was left to drive the bus and canoe racks to retrieve floaters downstream at Spawt Mill. It was a festive spot in a deep gorge, hillsides heavy with forest, the green broken in spots by bare rocks that lunged into view. A pale dam backed the river into a giant pool, a huge and perfect swimming hole, the dam low enough to sit on with feet swishing in the water. A narrow opening in the dam at the near bank let water push into the old mill trace, but the wheel didn't turn anymore. Morrow watched kids swing on a rope and flop into the river. Girls roamed on top of the dam, and young men followed at a slight distance, drinking beer, shoving one another around. Hawks dragged their shadows across the pool, fish jumped, and he was on this very spot at age fifteen, uncertain in all directions, gawking at a girl whose beauty stunned and terrorized him. She posed on the dam and didn't wear a swimsuit, but an ankle-length hippie shift of some sort, thin cloth rich with Eastern patterns, mystic cubes and squiggles, and nothing underneath. Light passed through the V of her legs so clearly he didn't have to guess. Maybe she hadn't intended to get wet, but walked the dam barefoot with the other girls until carried away by the view, the smell of river, the roiling of fresh water down the sluice to the mill, the roaring and the laughter. Morrow was as though paralyzed by her from first sight, and she noticed, smiled his way, and stopped in the overflow on the dam, doing dance steps that splashed, then dropped her shoulder and looked rearward again, a gesture he never got over. Her skin immediately sang to him of summer fun, perhaps endless summer fun, and her eyes were brown places to romp, revel, rejoice—hair to her waist and deep dimples that opened when she smiled. She waved to him and he turned away, anguished by his attraction to her and her nearness, all words flown from his head. When he turned back, she was in the river, swimming toward him in that hippie shift, hair spread on the water, trailing behind, her girlfriends watching with interest. She stepped out of the river, standing tall, boldly revealed by the soaked cloth, walking straight to him. He spun on the gravel and took off before she spoke, but heard her say, "Are you kidding?" as he hustled with his head down to the store in the old mill and found his parents. He spotted her when they left, lost his nerve again as she watched him from the pooled water, but that day released her into his emotions to stay—he'd carried her with him as a feeling more than a picture, a sunken feeling linked to all things lost or untried, but now he had her face again, blooming young and clear, that smile, the wonderful skin of July. He knew she would have been the beginner's romance

teens should have, need to have, deserve, a magical summer of smitten days with moments of exploratory bliss
that he could've savored all these years since, instead of
feeling wrecked by the pitiless regret that he'd been such
a no-balls virgin coward when confronted with what he
most desired.

He drank whisky that night, the first time since leaving Nebraska. So many of the campers had long tanned
legs and bare bellies, cute flaking noses, carefree laughter,
husbands fishing somewhere until dark. At the supper
hour he'd wandered between tents holding a paper cup of
scotch on the rocks, sipping, eyes reddening, speech beginning to limp, enjoying the casual company of women
who glowed and dressed for the heat. The sun was
snaking brightly along the ridgeline; kids were diving
from the bridge.

He returned to the store, called his oldest daughter at
school in Palo Alto, but went to voice mail and left a mes-
sage, "Don't be stingy to yourself, babe. Overall, I mean,
don't be...I'm fine." When he dropped the phone, Royce
took the cup from his hand and set it beneath the counter.
He said, "No misery gets sweeter dipped in devil juice,
Mr. Morrow. Looks like you got customers."

Out the window he saw a cloud of dust rise from the
parking lot and watched as it grew wider and higher and
spread over the nearest tents. People trying to eat or rest
started hacking in the cloud, spitting, shielding their eyes
as the dust swooped over them. The car was a sedan, a

dented beater, branch scrapes in the paint, mud blown to the door handles, and music blasted from inside. The driver cut figure eights, gunning the engine then slamming the brakes to slide and swerve until the dust cloud enveloped the store and all of the tents. People began to stand and shout before the car stopped. The cloud continued to rotate and obscure while the music played.

Morrow went down the steps, waving dust away, and approached the car. He could see four heads inside. "What the hell you think you're doing?"

The music was silenced. The engine ticked. The front doors squeaked when slowly opened. The driver said, "You cussin' at me?" Both men were tattooed in script and held machetes with arms that were stark and taut—long hair, narrow faces. The groans of women carried from the backseat. "I'ma cut you up'n down for cussin' me in front of bitches."

The other raised his machete, said, "We'll both of us cut on him."

The campers had quieted but stood watching, unmoving witnesses powdered by dust, and Morrow backed toward the front steps of the store. He said, "Just drive away. Get in and drive away."

"Not 'til I hack me a piece of you to take along."

"I've asked you to leave."

"That might mean shit to somebody, but..."

On the top step Morrow paused. His legs felt softened at the joints and waggled a little, and something inside had plunged. When he raised his hand toward the advancing men his fingers shook. "Just get," he said, but they kept coming, though not quickly, unsteady in their own legs, too. Royce eased up from behind and handed Morrow his bird gun, a twenty-gauge pump meant for quail and dove. He said, "Them boys are Langans—they ain't playactin'—you might need to shoot the two of 'em."

The women climbed from the beater and stood beside it, the elder subdued and expectant of the worst, the younger dark and expressionless, staring at Morrow. He looked back and could not believe how pretty her eyes were—what color is that?—then couldn't believe he'd noticed. He abruptly fired into the air while yet lost in her eyes and presence, and said, "One more step."

The men halted at the sound, looked at each other, laughed 'til they bent in the middle and had to lean together. The machetes fell to ground. The driver turned to the staring girl. "Toss me keys to the trunk."

Royce said, "Don't let them open that trunk. You won't want that."

"You open that trunk and I'll kill you." Morrow didn't know where these words were coming from, but he let them come, hoped for them to continue, wondered where they'd been all his life. He could feel her watching. "I'll shoot you where you stand."

The girl bent into the car and took the keys with her as she walked toward the bridge in plastic sandals and a dress that didn't fit her body or the season. She did not speak, but looked back at Morrow twice, glancing over her shoulder. She had muddy hands and unbridled hair, and her face suggested she'd yet to be pleasantly surprised by life.

The men stood beside the car, and the driver said, "Man, I'm diggin' your hole already in my head."

"Just don't move."

"I hope it's dug to fit you, 'cause you're goin' to be dead in it a long time."

"Lower your voice; you're scaring the children."

When the sheriff appeared at the top of the hill the driver fled into the woods. The other man sat on the dust and held his hands behind his back. The sheriff took charge, called the man by name as he hooked him into cuffs. The women gave short statements of no value, and the sheriff removed three long guns and a dynamite stick from the trunk before he let them drive away. He sidled near, hat in hand, and warned Morrow in whispers. As the sheriff and his prisoner departed, the crowd of campers burst into applause for Morrow, sincere clapping and broad smiles, before returning to their tents while telling slightly or largely different versions of what they'd all just seen.

The woods had grown dark and Morrow went inside, rested the shotgun against a handy wall. He began to shake in every limb and had to sit down. Kids stood in the doorway staring at him. He kneeled behind the counter and puked below the cash register.

Royce went to the utility closet and selected a mop. He stood in the shadow cast by the buffalo head on the wall, then shoved the mop into the mess and began to swab. He said, "Langan'll probably scramble over to his grandma's house. That's where he usually goes to hide. He may well have forgot about you by the time he gets there. But maybe not."

"You go on home," Morrow said. He stood and took the mop into his own hands. "I've got it."

That night he paced near the big window, watching for the man, keeping his bird gun near. Whenever headlights passed the store, he opened the door for a clear view. He paced and kept a lookout for the man, but was thinking of the girl, the girl he'd seen long ago and the girl he'd seen in the dust. Somehow they became the same girl; there was a blending of then and now, her and her, and a combination of fresh excitement and release kept Morrow awake until at dawn he leaned the shotgun against the tree his robe hung from, and dove into the river to swim upstream.

Florianne

If they ever catch who took my daughter, I'll probably know him. Maybe I've known him all my life; maybe he's only a familiar face and name. I might have given him credit at the store, let his tab ride till next Friday or the one after, carried groceries to the car for his wife, cut two pounds from a chub of bologna and shaved it paper-thin the way he likes. Maybe he leans on the counter and repeats his favorite jokes, and I laugh at the right parts while recalling the sound of his mitt snapping shut when he shagged fly balls long ago.

I suspect everybody around here and nobody special.

At the opening of each deer season I hope this time she'll be found. Eleven hunts have come and gone now, and others have been stumbled across in culverts, under old plywood, wrapped carefully in white sheets, and piled over with leaves, but not my girl. This is rough country, though, steep hills, rocky bottoms, hard ground to walk on, gloomy from the trees, and she could be ten feet away as three hunters pass and they'd all miss her. She might lie somewhere else, I guess, under a barn or the freshest patch of concrete in a bachelor's basement, but that's not how it comes to me. I can hear wind in the trees and limbs tapping limbs and feel rain.

She disappeared only a quarter mile down our road, taken out of the churchyard where she was mowing the grass, putting a few bucks in her pocket for Saturday night. There are exactly three homes between ours and the church and no strangers in any of them. The lawn mower was still running, blatting and fuming untended beside the tall stone church, until the nearest neighbor noticed the annoying noise no longer moved to and fro and looked from a window. She'd've turned seventeen in a month. There's never been another sign of her.

Sometimes I'll be at the cash register and catch somebody looking at me in a sort of funny way, at such a slant as to appear sneaky, or with lips curled too high on one end, and think, Is that him? Is he watching me sack groceries and gloating? Does that shifty glance say I fucked your daughter, Henry, from every which angle that felt good to me, then choked the light from her pretty eyes and put her... Should I grab him now while he's handy and beat on him till he tells me where I can rake her bones together?

At some point every old friend sensed my suspicion aim their way and several couldn't get over that moment of recognition, even after my suspicion rotated to the next ol' buddy, or slightly creepy cousin, that mailman with the pencil mustache. There was no blood, no hair strands snatched loose in a fight or torn bits of her blouse, and she was a strong girl, so he had a gun to her head or she trusted him enough to go sit in his truck a minute, hang out, sip a soda. That brings everybody I know into the picture.

Her mother ran west when the girl was five. I was too steady for her taste, too regular, too much the same one day to another. She wanted fizzy drinks and jukeboxes, different arms to hold her every week or two. She remembered her daughter's birthday for a few years, sent a gift at Christmas, then she just didn't anymore. She'd turned that page, lit a fresh cigarette, poured a cold one, found new lips to kiss.

I went to all the trouble and tracked her to Reno once our girl was gone, and she said, "Everything with you is a downer, Henry. I just can't stand your blah-blah-blah negative attitude. You're so selfish that way. She'll turn up."

"She didn't leave—she was taken."

"What's your proof? You got any?"

"You don't even know her."

The phone went click, and that was it. She has yet to call with another question.

I always wondered if her mom's leaving was why the girl ran to fat for so long, had a roly-poly figure until the year before she went gone. She took up swimming, jogging, some flowery-sounding yoga class at the Civic Center, ate salads and more salads and rice cakes. She made herself into a size she hadn't believed she could ever be. That meant so much to her, to finally have a figure clothes looked good on, to feel a little admired when lolling around the pool in town, wear shorts to the ballpark on summer nights.

I've often thought about that: If she'd stayed chunky would she be here now?

Such questions popping up keep the hurt fresh.

And sometimes I think, Were there two of them? Three?

How much of our world is in on this?

Black Step

The cow trembled in the sideways tree, the broken left foreleg canted in a separate direction from the other legs, snapped sharply to the right and dangling. There'd been moans since the storm in the night pushed on and away and the wind calmed. The cow heard my feet rustle pebbles on the cliff, and its tired neck raised the head to look up at me. The cow had wide screaming eyes that were saying things that living things say to me in that language better than words. That language that travels. I've seen it everywhere.

The sideways tree was a lonely old sycamore halfway down the cliff that grew straight out from the face for about ten feet, then curled upward for another thirty. Far below, the river flowed clean and dense in the morning shadow cast by the bluff, the rocks in its bed singing of centuries spent singing in the rushing, the things that wash by, bump going past, leave marks or bones. And the cow repeated everything again with those shrill eyes pointed my way, pleading as it had since the forest started rattling and lightning shanks stomped down yellow from the sky and the wind huffed 'til bad instincts took charge and the cow plunged through the barbed wire, seeking a way out of the suddenly terrifying pasture but found only a way down, and the sideways tree snagged it so it had a long hurt night held aloft to hear the rocks far, far below, and know horror.

I felt responsible for the cows.

I turned and walked across the broad sopping pasture toward Ma's house, tall supple grass flicking droplets to my knees. The sky had been washed baby blue and blank, and the other cows were munching away at the greenery, rubbing their hides on small trees. Ma's house is a square two-story built plain long ago and still sturdy. It's painted an invented shade of white about halfway around the house to where the paint ran out, just past the south corner and beyond sight from the road, some certain mix of various whites you have to fetch from town. The rest of the house has been colored with the paler paints left over in the shed, so it's one color house seen driving by, several others standing in the yard, colors that don't rhyme in the eye, but the old wood is well coated. A ladder yet leans there, and a couple of brushes on the bottom rung have stiffened atop a paint can lid.

She's asleep, Ma, snoring in her room, letting the creep of cancer slip her mind a spell, and I go tiptoe through the kitchen to the gun cupboard in the hall. The rifle I want is standing in the back now, behind a cracked oil lantern and a pile of yesteryear phone books, not handy like I kept it. It's an old bruiser, a bolt-action aught-six that has been whipped on by wintry thickets slapping and raw sporting weather since two grandpas ago, yet it still has a glow to it, a veteran allure. I trust this one most.

The cow screams at me again with those eyes. Screams what you think it would. The sideways tree is too far down the cliff for me to clamber there, even if I was willing. In the valley and downriver a short ways there's a twist of smoke coming from a new house I keep forgetting is there now. A strange but handsome riverside house made of fresh shining wood, with a steep roof of bluish tile, where outsiders have come to live. I stand on the cliff so a stray round won't pop into a tile.

This target seemed so close, so easy, so harmless, not like those when I'd been elsewhere.

I said, "Should've stopped at the checkpoint, hajji."

The dead cow slumped more loosely over the sideways tree. The eyes finally hushed. One leg strode hard for a few seconds, trying to climb the cliff now it was shot, climb the cliff in death, then abruptly stilled.

A man came out of the house below and stared at me, a

silver-haired man in a black T-shirt, until I flapped a hand his way that meant never mind, it's okay, and he nodded. He went about his business, stacking firewood in the yard, a dog trailing him, a cat trailing the dog, a woman standing on the porch. Together it all makes one of those pictures of perfect life that might splay across your mind when you are far off and think of home, somebody else's home, the kind that looks like that and raises your spirits.

In Ward 53, where they fretted about me so, they told me maybe I should paint, take up painting landscapes or portraits, something soothing, but whenever I try the picture explodes on me, the light of day shatters, the humans don't look too human, and strange patterns span the sky. Sometimes the sky is all cherry blossoms, one big blush of pink and white, and there's bones sticking up from the mud below, with little volunteer vines growing around them, linking them together, like the scattered bones don't truly belong to death but might hop up reunited by vines and dance a loose clattering jig once more. Hopeful, I guess, deep down, which is why they wanted me to paint.

I have a dozen dead items painted that way.

I know the departed cow in the sideways tree will be next.

Before I went into the desert I'd had a decent job at Spangler Feeds, hefting sacks, stacking salt blocks, sweeping grain dust and such, and they would've held it for me, but the whole feed mill burned down to a knee-high mess of ash and nails while I was away, and the Spanglers decided not to rebuild, just not worth it, so they moved to Florida instead and fish for big ones at sea a lot. They sent a postcard. Where Ma worked didn't help with insurance, so now I watch her cows for her while I can and we'll contribute the dough to cancer treatment.

Ma's a Boshell. I'm a Girard, because Ma got to feeling guilty after Dad was gone and had my papers fixed so I was legally his, even if they'd never married. Dad Dad, my sorrowful Dad, was a man given to long blue spells pierced by moments of excited yearning—a handsome doomed man I like more and more as the days roll past and I imagine him with dark curls and thin whiskers and how we resemble.

I carried the rifle with me and marched across the field counting cows. I had got to know them by their color schemes and shapes, and two or three were the kind of cows that had personalities, too, goofy traits or bad tempers that made them stand out among the herd. Only the one had bolted. I walked under the shade trees and around the wallow of red mud and dull water counting twice, then I went to the house to fetch my painting stuff, which they'd been very glad to give me back at Ward 53.

I set the easel above the cow, considered colors I might use, colors that'd catch the feeling of this killed cow, the tragedy of last night that was already nearly forgot, while the cliff and tree and bullet hole'd tell the facts of the story. The color of the actual cow meant nothing now, so I'd fit some to it—colors that suited would come about somehow as my brush moved, and the tree would get rendered the same. I sensed blue for the cow and bronze for the tree and blue again for the killing ground that waited below the tense yellow cliff. The sky grew plum and gray and rippled like a window curtain. As I made the picture, the scene in my head took over and the cliff turned up flat on me, so the plum-gray sky was standing sentry over to the right, and the cow in the sideways tree hung above level ground but below the branch, disobeying gravity now that it'd died.

The bullet hole was a pink question mark.

Ma had walked the pasture counting heads while I was lost deep inside that scene with the cow, and crept along behind me. I was adding chrome boulders to the stream, and when I caught a creeping sound behind I fast as a flinch reached for the rifle, but the rifle wasn't there, and I sprang for the dirt with one hand shielding my face while the other aimed the paintbrush. The brush swept back and forth, wanting to spray a wide field of fire, a death blossom, get 'em all, and I felt wiggly in my head as a few drops dove loose to dribble down me.

Ma said, "That cow's money lost now."

They tell me Dad committed suicide for reasons he dreamed up. His mind was too active. He had a round mind and it roamed. He could imagine any kind of hurt. He could imagine the many miseries of this world flying over from everywhere to roost between his ears, but he couldn't imagine how to get away. Ma loved him past his end and has never kissed another man. She loved his mind, his round, roaming mind that made her feel a glowing inside her skin between those spells of blight. He waited all of a calm spring night for some fresh serious pain to come into his heart and kill him. Twelve coiled hours hunched at the kitchen table, frozen peas dumped on the tabletop, a shotgun leaning against the back of his chair. He arranged rank after rank of cold green peas, took aim, and flicked each toward the kitchen sink and kept a secret score. Then he gathered the peas from the sink and floor, rearranged them across the tabletop, and flicked them all again. Once the peas were ruined, he switched to flicking corn kernels, raisins, whatever, until the score was lost in his head and the floor slippery. He drank enough coffee his brain shook in its bowl, then drank whiskey to get that shaky brain calm. At some point inside that addled calmness the heavy curtains parted and he thought he spied a good way out, an answer to it all—stepped to the back stoop and sat and erased his problems in this world, maybe not the next. He died gushing blood on the second step of the back stoop, the step we keep painted black.

I don't truly remember, but Ma has told me about it, made it meaningful to me, saying I followed him onto the stoop, my rusty diaper drooping, and the ejected shell bounced off my belly, and Dad tried to say one last word to me but it drowned in blood that jumped up in his throat, never got said. So now I do sort of recall an ejected shell bouncing from my baby-belly, blood flying, that one last word drowning in red.

He's buried out back, Buddy Girard, and Ma prays at his grave.

Ma? Ma? She's not all there; parts have fallen away and dashed, dashed against her days, parts that fell the day she was pulled from school at sixteen and sent to work at the shoe factory, parts that fell the day the shoe factory closed, the day Marcella died in her crib, the day she was told she had cancer, the day Dad died on that one black step. She has always carried on, though, Ma, hefting the parts of herself that remained, dragging them onward, and remaining more decent than she had to be, which makes me try to stay alive for her.

Ma wants to be buried on the farm. She'd been happy here when she was too young to know better and during the first year with Dad. Her grave will be near the rest, but not quite with them, several paces to the west of the others, under the dirt with Buddy. I've squared the plot with railroad ties, and we've planted perennials along the border, purple phlox and daisies and such that wave spirited colors when a breeze passes. The graves overlook the river and are well shaded in summer until about noon, then the good light reaches and grows things there. A spot has been picked for me, also, to the sundown side, and I've found my marker, a reddish river stone with battered edges and a kind of cracked, silent dignity. It's too big to throw or kick away. The stone will remain unchanged, no name or date, and someday vines and flowers will cover the stone in tangled green and sweetness. Ma wants a regular wooden cross about three feet tall, painted white, same as Dad had before a high wind flung his away.

You have to know where to stand to stand over his grave.

I like graves that disappear.

Mary is the woman who has chosen me to be the man she needs. She has rooted inside my life and claimed me, claimed me to be her man of tomorrow and the days after, claimed me for loving, too, I guess. She lives with her momma four miles away, near where Chime Creek joins the Twin Forks, in a trailer with her kids, two of them, Joe and Nora, neither old enough for school but both already hunkered down into a fretful shyness, a reluctance to be noticed or speak up. Mary likes to visit me after dark, once the bars have got boring, raise dust driving her heavy rattling car into Ma's yard, and park under the spreading oak, radio music kicking holes through the night quiet.

She grunts getting out of the car, slams the door. Most times she'll have a movie in her hand, whatever beer is left tucked under her arm. Her moccasins are silent crossing the dirt.

This time, same as always, I greet her with "Mary."

"Yup. Once again." She's taller than she wants to be and rolls her shoulders forward to shorten her neck, drops her chin, sags her upper self like a flower that's got a blooming too heavy atop for its stem to carry. She holds the movie toward me, shakes the box. "How 'bout a picture show, Darden?"

"Funny?"

"Could be to you."

Mary wants to kiss, so I do, and she wants some sort of familiar caress, one that suggests we know each other's bodies like favorite getaway places we've come to own, so I put both hands to her butt and pull the cheeks spread a little bit, lift her. Mary has a small beer pooch underslung from her lower belly, but is elsewhere lean, skinny, even, and I can about feel the bone under her butt with my fingertips. She's got pale hair and a few freckles that seem to be forever fading from her face but never go away.

In the living room she right away wants me to get naked. Ma's bed is downstairs so she can be near the john, and she lays snoring in the dining room, just around the corner. The TV is muted but on, throwing a headache light across the room, throbbing between near dark to suddenly glaring, with many skittish flickers between. I know I'm supposed to want this, what she offers, so I try to recall how it goes when this is something you want, crave, gotta have, can't do without, might kill for, die over, mourn when it's gone.

54

Somehow my clothes come off, drop to the floor, first frost stripping a tree of its last clinging leaves.

"Such a tight, smooth boy," she says. Mary is pushing nine years older, and unlike most women would do she apparently enjoys reminding me I'm way younger. It somehow stokes her needs and juices her good to say it aloud. Whenever she says it she sighs soft and looks like a crouched cat studying songbirds in a low bush. "Lucky ol' me. Lucky, lucky."

All Mary does is scoot from her moccasins and jeans and blue undies. She keeps her shirt on and buttoned, the tails hanging over that pooch. Her lips get around on me some, visiting here and there, then I bend her over the couch, knees to the carpet, and slam her the doggy-way she wants it most times. Slap her ass as she has taught me while I slam, slam and slap, and she snickers, snickers, moans into the cushions. Fresh rug burns get added to the old on my knees and I collapse backwards after, stare at the ceiling, count the cobwebs and get the same tally as the visit before.

She says now I'm home for a while we should get married, and soon, before they send me back, but has only ever one time asked me about over there, how it was, what details I needed to get off my chest, what memories I might want to share with her, and I said, It's all real sandy. Sand blows into everything. Makes soup even turn crunchy.

That's it?

I think I miss the crunching.

"Put this in," she says before my breathing is even righted, and tosses the movie my way. She raises herself to sit on the couch, then uses her blue undies to mop herself dry, catch my come seeping, and stuffs them dampened into her purse. "It's got that guy in it I like."

Somewhere in the flick I fell out of interest. It wasn't funny, and the guy she liked so dodged bullets slower than pigeons and cracked wise at death, which never happened to him or his, and I yawned and went away. On the porch I stared up at the big oak in the yard. Tree frogs honked their raspy honks in unison, and fat brown bugs battered the porch light behind me. Mary's car was under the spread limbs, and I saw that the windows had fogged. I crossed the dirt yard, opened the back door, and there slept Joe and Nora, undressed for bed but without a blanket to cover them. I pointed a finger and wrote Mary's name in the fog above them, then rubbed their used wet breaths onto my face. They'd been there since she left the trailer and hit the first bar, and were probably asleep by the second roadhouse or the third. I picked both up at once, an arm under each, and neither child woke as I carried them inside. Mary looked over from her movie as I laid the kids on the empty end of the couch. She was smiling with her chin down and her eyes wide, and said, "See? I told you you loved them kids."

* * *

In the story that happens to me so often, asleep or wide awake, I had got down on my hands and knees to collect red and white parts of Lt. Voorhees, from when his brain-housing unit came apart in his quarters, skull chunks denting the ceiling, teeth and ears splatted to the walls, brains a clotting spray—a story that happens to me whenever it wants to, and I can't shunt it aside or stuff it in a box, but can only accept the sunken feelings it deals me time and again. A few times Dad showed up to help me collect the cracked bone and stringy glop, clumped hair, kneeling beside me in a foreign place, calling me "son" while we raised a wet pile. Some days I start hearing the final words Lt. Voorhees said before closing his door that night spoken over and over, at different volumes in my head, all day long, low to loud, Hope I dream about daylight again.

Hope I DREAM about daylight AGAIN.

HOPE I dream about DAYLIGHT again.

McArdle and Fuller fell by toward the next sundown, or the one after, drawn by boredom and word of my return, wanting to remember high school, with a box of beer and bowls of smoke to make it seem those years-ago days might happen again tomorrow if only we got wasted enough. I left the house with them in McArdle's truck and we drove to the river, built a jolly campfire on a gravel beach. Their memories are cleaner than mine, the silly details yet shine for them, are easily found and spoken as jokes or boasts. My head cramps trying to only call up the faces from the hallways. I should be glad for this visit, I know, so I hunt dry wood up the slope, stack it on the fire to grow the flames, and say I am, I am glad to see you two, your faces make me feel home.

So-and-so got married, so-and-so moved away, so-and-so fell in the lake or was pushed, drunk as a skunk whichever. It takes only five minutes together before they lean close and ask the standard ghoul questions I expect from civilians, and I answer, Oh, you damned straight I did.

Then, Maybe more'n used to ride our school bus.

Then, Like tomatoes being busted open with hammers.

Then, Sometimes all you can do is shovel red sand into a body bag and send that home with a name on it.

The empties clatter into the fire, smokes mingle, dusk settles, there is laughter. I recall times together like this, drinking the day away in canoes on the river, chucking dry-ice bombs into blue holes and cheering the boom and spray, and as dark fell driving into town with more cold beer to circle the Sonic, round and round at half a mile an hour, biceps on display out the windows, hoping some town girls would of a sudden realize we were cute, kind of sexy, even, and want to go for a ride in the country, then switching to whiskey when none did.

I guess I joined to become more interesting than that.

Fuller had been our alpha, our main instigator, with showboat muscles and a habit of bruising you good in horseplay, then saying it was only a joke, bro, don't be mad. In the firelight I can see he'd like to mess with me some again, as he did back when, give a demeaning Dutch rub, or clamp on a headlock 'til I croak "Uncle," but he's just not sure anymore, not sure I won't go Kill! Kill! Kill! in my head, yank something deadly from my watch pocket, zip-cuff him to a sapling, and feed his ass to the fire a pound at a time. I can see the itch is in him, and the doubt, so I help him clear the confusion, saying, "After the desert, bro, the list of things you're totally certain you'd *never ever do* gets a lot shorter."

Ma's breaths scrape together traveling her throat and have short hisses at their tail, plus something come undone in her chest clatters. Her sleep is a busy place and she speaks mushed words into the sheets, her legs walk to yesterday and back across the mattress, her eyelids totter as the eyeballs rush about in darkness, wanting to see everything they've ever seen again. The bed she chose for the dining room is small with no headboard, low to ground, a short fall if she rolled loose in her rambling and tumbled.

Another rough day before noon there was this cemetery in the sand, with row after row of markers for the dead, mud-colored or white, each big enough to hide behind, and a high dun wall around the whole place. We cleared one row then crept toward the next, each small distance electric with the idea that this gravestone

ahead could be the one Ali Baba is hid behind and waiting, finger on the trigger or arm cocked to throw something that explodes. The air smelled of shit roasting in
oil and carried that shrill music that made your skin
tighten. One row at a time, crawling inch by inch, from
marker to marker, the pressure building with each scoot
forward, sweat dripping, hands turned white squeezing,
and after several rows you heard some guys go empty,
moan themselves into the dust, become still where they
were, not about to move on. They make it ten, twenty,
thirty rows, but can no longer imagine making it through
all the rows. Each marker, each row, who knows what's
there, anything could be, you might soon become a
chunky breeze exploded sideways or get shot through-
and-through, and those possibilities nourished dread.
Your own mind can gut you good so easy. With sprung
nerves soldiers lay faces to the sand to avoid seeing ahead
and had to be booted by sergeants.

Mary wanted to be a bride again and announced she soon
would be while we all splashed in the river. Joe and Nora
hopped on stick legs in the shallows above the one-lane
bridge, and Ma sat in a folding chair with her feet under
water and a scarf over her fuzz of hair. I had my goggles
to hunt treasure spilled from tourist canoes upstream and
had found a wristwatch with a rotted band. Mary wore a
white T-shirt over her suit and said, "It's official, y'all—
me'n Darden are gettin' hitched."

I dove again. People riding inner tubes went by over-head, casting squat shadows that roamed over the bottom rocks and stretched with distance. Legs looked so white and puffed from underneath, with bubbles attaching to the flesh like blisters, and voices arrived as deep blurry barks.

Ma said, "When does this happen?"

"While he waits to hear about goin' back," Mary said. The sun was halfway west and shined at a slant that broke around her. Her face was shaded faint but the skin on her neck glowed at the sides. "I'll get it right this time. I've learned some things I couldn't've guessed at before."

Joe and Nora stood still in a trickle of river, bare feet sinking into the gravel bed, staring at me, faces empty, holding themselves in tight. Mary saw and kicked water at them so they'd know it was okay to seem happy just now. They tried.

Mary unloaded a picnic onto a blanket in the shade, beer chilling in the river.

Ma said to me, "You sure this is good news?" Her eyes were mournful and ringed, like those of a hunted thing that has decided to stop running. I would paint her soon. Her chest had been cut away from her first, both sides, but she fell sick in other parts, too, and the sick didn't rest; it prowled her body, salting her with ruin you couldn't see in her face for a good long while. Now the ruin just stares out at me, all the time, from those eyes that know about hope and that body that can't offer any. She leaned my way and whispered, "It's your life, son."

"I just don't care to make big decisions anymore."

"That is one."

"Let's act happy."

"That's another."

I fell on the river and went inside. The water ran chest deep, and I spread over the rocky bottom and found a big one to cling to. There were all these tiny tatters of different debris rushing past near the bottom and the rushing was all I heard. I clung to the bottom, my feet rising behind and touching air while my hands held steady on the slickened old stone and kept me from spinning downstream. I held and held to the rock and forgot about breathing, sunk into that choice spot between breathing and not ever breathing, between raising up to walk on the bank and picnic or staying under to join that debris already lost to the rushing.

Stink from the cow took over the air. The cow was screaming again, screaming stink, a brown dirge of stink like the dead scream always. Ma and me stood on the cliff with our noses pinched against the loud stink and squinted our eyes, too. Ma's trying to act spry so she can help. She's wearing rubber mud boots and a long dress with no waistline and no pattern in the cloth. A big yellow sun hat shades her face.

Neither of us wants the cow kicked to the river below,

to dump such ruin into the clean water, so we decide to haul it up the cliff with three ropes. I've backed the truck near the edge, and Ma swears she can work a clutch and drive just fine, no problem. I tied my ropes to the truck, cinched one around me snug, and led the other two down to the sideways tree. There were shrubs to grab at on the cliff face, untrustworthy roots and clumps of stranded weeds, and I tossed my feet at them to slow my falling. The sideways tree was sturdy and the cow oozed. Flying things had got the eyes, the lips and ears, the soft easy meat anything left dead in the open serves up first. I had to sit astride the cow to get the ropes looped around, the first under the front legs, the next under the back, and thickened death-juices leaked from the cow onto my jeans and shirt. I gave Ma a wave and me and the cow scraped the dusty cliff and flew up together, meat and meat under the sky, hooves whirling, boots whirling, one head down, one head raised, one spinning smell.

Ma helps me unlash and says, "You're nuts to go back."

"They cleared me for goin', Ma."

Ma drove and the cow slid across the pasture to the grassless place, and I untied it. My clothes stunk past cleaning, and I flung them off, shirt first, then jeans, and went about in my skivvies and started tossing stuff from the trash heap into the burn circle. The pile grew, and grew tall enough for a ten-foot flame to rise from household trash, old plywood, a tangle of blowdown, hedge trimmings, a busted headboard and stained mattress I couldn't recall. I was near naked in the world and sweating, bending to drop matches, encourage the flames, scorch that stink away. Ma watched me, looking at my tats some, not too impressed by the pictures, I knew, but mostly studying the long ragged divot torn top to bottom on my back and wondering what invention made that wound.

"She found out how much you're worth dead."

"Where?"

"She's been askin' folks all around."

We stood close together fireside, watching the cow burn in the circle as the sun sank. The cow only slightly thinned, but the brain-housing unit was soon laid bare and white atop deep glowing coals. Hooves cracked in the heat. Full dark made fire seem the center of all things. A breeze raised little flames that wiggled in the eye sockets and stuck a long tongue of fire lapping from the mouth. Ma'n me stared silently 'til the tree frogs went quiet and owls came out to fly. We left the cow at peace finally in the embers, started toward the house, walking slowly through the spreading weeds of our garden plot where nothing got planted this year.

Night Stand

Pelham came awake one night to find a naked man standing over his bed, growling. There was little light in the bedroom, but he could see one arm of the man from his shoulder to his wrist, a grim tattoo of something burning, a pale suggestion of bared teeth and taut lips. The growling was menacing and confused, with shrill rises, deep ferocity giving way to brief keening trills, a mangle of tones. Jill woke, too, looked at the man, then rolled from bed and fled screaming toward the next room. Pelham reached for the light on the nightstand but his fingers rattled a plate that shouldn't have been there, and on the plate there lay a knife. The man stood still at the bottom of the bed, noisy and tall, a looming shadow inside the house that Pelham had to stand and fight, do what he could, stall for time and let Jill run, hide somewhere, since she must be what he's after—why else would he be naked? But the man made no move to chase her, and didn't lunge or leap onto Pelham like he could've, either, didn't take control and clobber him senseless, but only stood there growling with his arms at his sides, hands held low, and Pelham quick got to him with the blade, planted steel in his chest. A popping sound came from inside the man's ribs, and Pelham expected to be sliced in return now, maybe shot, but the man missed somehow, so close but he missed, and Pelham whipped in another stab and there came that plonk sound of striking a knothole hammering a nail, and the blade hung up in the ribs. The growls were weaker and calmer as Pelham twisted the blade, weaker and calmer, then the man's arms collapsed onto Pelham, damp hands clasping Pelham's shoulders as if to steady himself, hold himself upright, prevent himself from falling, and blood jumped from the chest wound, ran warm down Pelham's belly. The ribs let the knife loose of a sudden and the overhead light flicked on as Pelham aimed the blade and he saw the man in a bright clear flash, a big handsome kid, shaved head, too many tats, his chest hole leaking breath and bubbling blood, but his hand didn't halt. The kid's neck burst open beneath his chin, Jill screamed again, hot flung blood in the eyes blinded Pelham as the kid's arms squeezed about him, hugged him near, hugged him as they both fell to the floor and fell apart.

Blind yet, eyeballs rolling in the warm puddling, Pelham groped for a bedsheet. The kid's bare feet were slapping the wood floor, slapping down hard like he was clambering to the crest of a hill that wasn't there. Pelham blotted the blood from his eyes. Jill was weeping. The kid soon stilled, blue eyes open, footprints in red all around his body. The wind inside him escaped from ass and mouth. He never had said a word.

For weeks to come Pelham would wonder how that knife came to be on the nightstand. How did a knife that shouldn't have been there happen to be there on this particular night? He tried to recall the preceding days backwards from the killing moment, to unravel the hours and find that knife. He didn't eat before sleep anymore, acid reflux, so it wasn't there to carve apples or slice cheese. They'd had guests a couple of nights ago, though, a few friends in for an evening of bourbon and smoked turkey, and he'd gone to bed pretty well lit—had he craved a snack to soak up the sour mash, fuck the reflux, and fallen asleep before fetching any? There was no sign of food on the empty plate. They'd gone after trout on the Spring River the day before that, fog in the bottoms and rainbows filling their creels—maybe he'd meant to fix something rent in the gear? Cut a tangle loose, trim a fly, fix a net, or perform some other mysterious household task he simply could not recall.

The house became crowded with cops. Pelham lived amidst woods and pastures, but the city limits had recently expanded to make him a West Table resident, so it was town cops in uniform and out clomping about, huddling to look down at the kid, studying the mess across the floor. Pelham sat on the bed with Jill beside him. He'd shook and shuddered for a while, waiting on the cops, trying not to look at the wounds, the open eyes and footprints, but having a surprise feeling sneak up on him, a creepy congratulatory glee, an animal gloat— Hey, I was attacked by a nameless intruder, fight to the finish, my foe now lays slain, a righteous kill. Sometimes a man will dream about a moment like this, an opportunity for sanctified violence, a time to open the cage and allow the sleeping thing inside out to eat its fill. A cop in a plaid shirt and Cardinals cap said, "Where'd his weapon fall to?"

"It was dark."

"What'd he have?"

"Look under the bed, maybe."

"You know, he shit on your leather chair downstairs."

The leather recliner was Pelham's inheritance, his father's most cherished possession, and the shit was loose spatter and spread over the seat, one armrest. Two days later Pelham would give up trying to clean the leather, clean it enough to forget the spatter, and dragged the chair to the curb for the trash haulers to collect. Before nightfall he'd watched from the window as a man and two children pulled to the curb, checked the leather chair over, then excitedly jammed it into the trunk of their car and hurried away, grinning with the trunk lid bouncing. That was the first time Pelham caught himself speaking aloud to empty rooms, leaning against the window, watching his father's chair disappear. "And fuck you for making me kill you."

The cop said, "We found it outside, around the corner of the house, beside that big shrub. An ol' single-action pistol. His clothes were there, piled nice, really, and the pistol was underneath. A pocketknife, too. His wallet's got military ID in it, says his name is Randall Davies—know him?"

"I went to school with a guy named that."

"Well, this one was a junior."

The first time Pelham heard himself threatened was early that evening, in a convenience store when he and Jill went to buy more cleaning supplies. The bedroom floor was hardwood and the biggest puddle left an outline of blood that had settled into the grain like a birthmark and wouldn't come off easily. There was only one other customer, a man in a green shirt with his name sewn above the heart pocket, and he was whispering with the clerk. Pelham and Jill came to stand behind him, holding scouring powder and Murphy soap and scrub pads. They heard the words "killed, stabbed like a hog in autumn" and knew they were under discussion. They remained silent, didn't say a word, waited for the man to leave. As he left, the man spoke more loudly, "I been friends with that boy all his life, and if the law don't do right to the son of a bitch, I know who will." Jill started crying again on the way home, and when he pulled into the driveway she said, "Maybe that last stab could've been skipped, hon. The neck one."

He was called to the police station the next morning. The sky was rumbling, stuffed with dark clouds, but only a thin sheen fell, raising oil slicks on the streets, shining the grass. The cops were named Olmstead and Johnson and led him to a private office. The room was painted a neutral sort of white, like the room could hold no opinions about anything one way or the other, and there was a tape recorder on the table. Olmstead said, "You're certain sure you never did know him?"

"I could've seen him somewhere, but I don't recall it."

"His daddy knows who you are."

"From school days."

"And Jill, now, it couldn't be she'd got acquainted with such a handsome young fella somewhere, could it?"

"He was kinda young, man, but thanks a shitload for putting that thought in my head."

"So she might've?"

"Fuck you."

Pelham had killed before. He'd been on Okinawa waiting to turn eighteen, a lance corporal, and the day after his birthday made him eligible for combat he was herded into a fat airplane and taken to Saigon. He didn't know what was going on when he landed in Vietnam and didn't when he left, either. Jarheads hanging around a gedunk, waiting for assignment, and a corporal told them they were lucky men; they were going to someplace in the south where there wasn't much action to worry about. Everybody relaxed, tried to eat noodle soup with odd spoons they couldn't make work, and wrote postcards home expressing relief or disappointment. The radio started crackling about noon, and more and more senior men gathered to listen as the next hour passed. Suddenly the corporal said they weren't going where he'd thought, get on your feet. First chopper ride, a little airsick, flying north to a place under attack, a place with a name Pelham never did hear straight. They took fire coming in and two marines were hit and spread on the bulkhead. Pelham had blood on his face before he'd even landed at this place with a name he didn't know. A harried captain acknowledged the fresh arrivals with an irritated wave, and a sergeant sent the Fucking New Guys downhill to the foxholes nearest the wire. Rainwater deepened in the holes; drizzle never stopped. The hills were steep and richly green; fog was alive and lowering until dark. There was a sniper everybody kept yelling about. Pelham did not know where he'd been sent or who he was with. The only name he'd caught was of a marine who'd died on the way in, Lazzaro from Texas. He did not have a clear idea about the shape or size of the base. He was mightily afraid he might shoot the wrong target in the dark, but he didn't want to be hesitant. He didn't know which way to run if it came to that or whose name to scream seeking help. Enemy troops breached the wire twice that night. Mortar rounds made the mud fly. Pelham shot and shot and shot every shadow that came near or seemed like it might. When he next understood where he was, he lay in a white bed on a hospital ship with a humming in his head that didn't fade until he was home again. Sometime during his recovery he received the Purple Heart as a parting gift.

He'd served in Vietnam less than twenty-four hours and felt uncomfortable even mentioning that he'd been there, since other veterans always asked, Remember Mama something-or-other's joint on the road to Marble Mountain? Di di mau? Beans-and-motherfuckers? The way the gals in black pajamas'd yank one leg up high and pee out the side? No no no no. You're a bullshitter, then, 'cause if you were there, Jody, you'd know them things. A year after his return Pelham ceased to mention Vietnam to new acquaintances, dropped it from the biography of himself he'd give if asked. Only those who knew him before he went were certain that he'd gone. Jill was a second wife, fifteen years his junior, a lovely, patient blonde, and remembered Vietnam as a tiresome old television show that'd finally been cancelled about the time she left third grade. She touched Pelham's scars but didn't ask for details.

That weather, that look, a forest in fog, a faint drizzle and no sky, always took him back to his foxhole in a place he couldn't name. Such weather often lay over the

mountain rivers where he and Jill went fishing, and the
next time they went the sky spread low and gray over the
bottoms and he could smell foreign mud and old fear. Jill
stood knee-deep in the flow, facing upstream from Pelham all morning, silent and tense, then finally turned
downstream and said, "No. No, I never did."

For two days they received threats by telephone, and
Pelham would listen to the harsh plans for his body
parts and sorry soul and quietly say, "You might be
right, man, come on over." A car drove by a couple of
times with young voices screaming something unintelli-
gible but loud and angry. Then a long follow-up article
in the town paper made the facts of the case obvious
and nobody much blamed Pelham anymore. A day later
there was an obituary of Randall Davies Jr.—a lifelong
member of the Front Street Church of Christ, avid quail
hunter, top rebounder on the West Table High basketball
team, best buddy to his sisters Chrystal and Joy, a proud
member of the First Marine Expeditionary Force in Iraq,
where he attained the rank of corporal, beloved of many.
Jill taped the obit to the refrigerator door so they might
slowly come to understand something crucial from regularly looking into the kid's face.

If they snacked at the small kitchen table, the face
would be above and between them. It was his boot camp
photograph, him wearing dress blues, the white hat and
brass insignia, a blank, regimented expression. They'd
watch the face as they sliced their food and chewed.

Studying that face forced the conversation into certain directions. Pelham might ask yet again, "Why ever'd he leave his weapons outside?"

"And why come in here naked?"

"Why shit on Daddy's chair? Why do that?"

"Contempt, hon. I think that means contempt."

"He never even threw a punch."

When Pelham cursed aloud in empty rooms, he knew he was talking to the marine he'd killed. He thought of him as Junior, and interrogated him in his mind, sometimes shook or slapped him. How'd you happen to pick my door? This road is not the route to anywhere special, Junior, ain't no popular taverns, or skating rinks, or Lovers' Lanes, or anything out this way—you've got to want to get here to get here. Junior never answered, and Jill was unnerved when she came upon Pelham standing in the living room addressing a closet door, "Fuck you! Fuck you! Fuck you!"

"Hon? Hon?"

"I'm after answers, that's what."

In the night Pelham would rise from bed and patrol the perimeter. He'd sneak through his house in his underwear, carrying an ax handle he'd brought in from the garage. He'd check doors, listen for sounds that might not be benign, creep to a window and peer between the blinds, stand at the empty spot where his father's chair belonged, with the ax handle drawn back to swing. He'd repeat his patrol several times in succession before relaxing a bit, and at some point Jill usually joined him in the darkness.

"All clear?"

"Maybe."

On a bright morning outside Kenny's Walleye Restaurant, Pelham finally bumped into Randall Davies Sr. He stood in the parking lot and felt great relief. Randall and his wife stared a moment, then Randall said, "I thought you'd come by before now."

The men started to shake hands, then stalled, averted their glances, let their hands fall to their sides. Mrs. Davies stepped forward, a tall and very thin woman who'd been several grades behind the men in school, and said, "I know you had the right—but I just can't look at your face. I just can't do it." She walked to Kenny's and went inside, and Randall raised his hand again, and this time they shook. He said, "She can't stand knowin' how wrong things got to be with him. How lost to us."

"I didn't know your son."

"Me, neither, much. I guess that's the awful part that's got so clear now."

"I'm sorry what happened happened."

"You'n me need to talk. I'll give you a call."

The summer they'd been buddies fell between grades six and seven. They'd roamed the fields and deep woods, taunted bulls in green pastures, mocked girls on the town square, dawdled in the alleyways where interesting refuse might be found. The Davieses were new arrivals, moved down from Rolla, and Pelham's mother told him to be nice to the freckled boy in thick glasses. Randall was not so hot at sports, but he was willing, and they joined other kids at the park for long, long games of corkball, Indian ball, 500, or, if their numbers swelled, double-headers of baseball with complete teams. They swam in Howl Creek, played slapjack on the screened porch when it rained, drank cream soda, and pegged rocks at pigeons in the empty railroad station. It was their last barefoot summer. Seventh grade brought many complications and new social concerns. Randall was of no help buttering up girls at the drive-in, or during a ritual scrap behind the school, more of a burden, really, a chronic liability, and before long, somehow, they didn't hang around to-gether anymore. Nothing angry happened, just a slow dwindling, and soon their friendship had shrunk to a glancing, rote exchange of greetings when passing: "How you doin'?"

"Not bad—you?"

"Can't kick."

Perfect weather pushed up from Arkansas, and all windows were open to the screen. Jill seemed buoyant and wore only a sheer light-blue nightie. The house breathed that night in the cadence of cicadas, drawing in the smells of honeysuckle and plowed dirt, dogwood and cattle in the distance. Pelham watched the final innings from St. Louis on the bedroom television, a tumbler of bourbon in his hand. Jill lay across the bed, face over the edge, book on the floor, the nightie smoothed to her skin. She snapped the book closed and sat up. "That one's over."

The announcer was praising the relief pitching, and Jill went to the bookcase, removed an aged hardback, and started moaning, then sniffling. "What?" he asked, and she pointed at the bookshelf where blood had flown and hidden behind the books, streaking the white paint. "Shit." Pelham fetched a bucket of water and cleaning rags, the stiff brush that worked best, and they cleared the books from the shelf, stacked them on the floor. They scrubbed and scrubbed until the paint flaked and that streaking of blood was gone from sight. Pelham dropped the brush into the bucket and said, "I'll be going to the river with his dad."

They stood on big gray rocks and cast into the current. Shallows began just below the men, and the river murmured passing over the small stones and limestone gravel. Shadows covered the riverbed and halfway up the slope beyond. The current tugged the fishing line like there was a bite and made the rods bend, but the only things on the line were the river and the bait. Randall spoke with his back to Pelham. "What'd Randy say to you?"

"Not a word. He never spoke."

"How is it you had a knife ready when he showed?"

"He only growled."

"I can't feature that part. I don't get that. I guess I just don't know what kind of shit really goes on over there."

"It's the same shit as always, Randall."

Pelham broke from the stream and stepped to the riverbank. He reached into his knapsack and retrieved a bottle of bourbon, then hopped back onto the gray rocks. He held the bottle toward Randall. "You ever start drinkin' whiskey?"

"Only had to start once."

They sat on the rocks, listening to the river, drinking bourbon from the bottle, letting trout swim past. They sat in silence for ten minutes, twenty, slowly sharing the whiskey. Two kids in yellow kayaks whipped down the channel, racing each other and laughing, easily skirting boulders and skimming the shallows. Their young laughter could yet be heard when they'd floated from sight, far downriver.

"He got different. He was always kind of lonely, you know, not so sure how he stood in the world, always lookin' for somehow to measure himself, prove somethin', figure what size of man he was. Could be he found out and it broke him."

"Randall—why me?"

"You know, he was plenty spooky sometimes—that stare, the hours'n hours when he wouldn't talk. I could see he was hurtin' in some way I never had to know, and he drank vodka in bed of a mornin' with his boots on and took other stuff, too, right there in the house. So, anyhow, one time I went in there while he stared at the ceiling with his boots on the sheets, and asked him, 'Son, you want to talk about it?' And he looks at me like he ain't certain sure we've met before, but he says, 'Will do, bro. Here's all your main answers: Yes. I lost count. Like tossin' a bucket of chili into a fan. Pick up all you can, shovel the rest.' "

"There it is." That very phrase took Pelham back to a time of rain. He screwed the cap onto the bottle and stood. He stretched his legs and turned upstream. He didn't want to tremble facing Randall. He jumped from the rocks and crouched at the water's edge, dunked his head and the cold sluiced through him and soaked his neck, drained down his spine. "Whiskey came a little early for me today."

"Me, too."

"Let's go."

That night Pelham taped his own boot camp photo onto the refrigerator, side by side with Junior's. Jill looked into the teenage face of her husband and asked, "Is that even you? You looked like that?"

His head was shaved, skin lightly reddened, hat set too squarely, a slight bruise puffed beneath his left eye, expression flat and unblinking.

"For a while, there, I looked exactly that way."

"Huh. I thought everybody was against Vietnam back then. That's all you ever hear about, anyhow. 'Hell no, we won't go,' that sort of stuff."

"That wasn't our neighborhood."

He studied the two faces and drank a beer, then another. Jill was mostly at the counter, chopping chicken parts to marinate for guests coming by tomorrow. Citrus and garlic smells were strong. He could see something happening to both faces, that relinquishing of who you'd been replaced by reflexive obedience, a new familiarity with exhaustion. They'd grill dinner and avoid this topic, probably, maybe drink too much just to hear the laughter. He wouldn't want guests to notice the photos, so he pulled them from the refrigerator, careful not to tear the edges, and held both in his hands. He switched the photos from one hand to the other, then back again. Jill became curious and stepped near, smelling of tomorrow, and looked over his shoulder.

"*Why* did you join again?" she asked, but didn't wait for an answer.

Pelham stepped outside, onto the wooden deck. A big moon cut shadows from everything and flung them around. He laid the photos on a lawn chair, then pulled his shirt over his head and dropped it on top of them. Then he slipped from his shoes, dropped his jeans and skivvies, and stood naked near the rail. He leaned on the wood, tried an experimental little growl. The next growl was more sincere; the one after that was louder. Pelham stood upright and breathed deeply, spread his arms wide, growled and growled toward the perimeter, inviting shadows to cross his yard.

"Hon?"

Two Things

When she comes over it is in a rattly old thing. Color yellow it got white-ring tires that rhyme the way round and the exhaust has slipped loose and is dragging sparks from it. There are stickers from the many funny places she been to on the bumper and two or three of her ideas are pasted on the fenders. A band-aid that look just like a band-aid only it is a monster has been momma'd onto the hood like the rattly old thing got some child sore in the motor.

Now this official had mailed us a note that tell Wilma who is the woman who is my wife and me that this lady wants to visit. It seems she teach Cecil something useful at the prison.

The door flings out and she squats up out of the car

coming my way. I have posted myself in the yard and she come straight at me smiling. Over her shoulder is a strap that holds up a big purse made of the sort of pale weeds they have in native lands I never saw.

She call me Mister McCoy right off like who I am is that clear-cut. Her name Frieda Buell she go on then flap out a hand for me to shake. I give her palm a little rub and tell her she is welcome.

When I see that sits with her good I tell her to come into the house.

That is something she would love to do she tells me.

This is a remark I don't believe so I stand back and inventory her. She is young with shaggy blond hair but she knows something about painting her face as she has done it smashing well. Her shirt is red and puffy and her shoes have heels that tell me walking is not a thing she practices over much. Her britches are pale and slicked onto her booty like they started as steam puffs.

The porch has sunk down so it hunkers a distance in front of the house. I ask her to be careful and she is. Inside I give her the good chair but I keep standing.

Right away I tell her I want to know what this about.

What it is about is a lulu. My son Cecil is a gifted man she says. He has a talent that puts a rareness to the world or something along those lines.

Cecil? Cecil a thief I tell her. And not that sly a one neither.

Once was she says. No more.

Always was. My mind is made up on that. But what's got me puzzled is what is this rareness he puts to the world or whatever?

Poetry is her answer. She reach her hand that has been overdone with various rings into the big purse and pulls out a booklet. She says Cecil has written it and the critics have claimed him as a natural in ability.

I take the booklet in my hands. It is of thick dry paper and the cover says "Dark Among the Grays" by Cecil McCoy. That is him all right I say. Tell me do this somehow line him up early for parole?

It could she says. She trying to face me bold enough but her eyes is playing hooky on her face and going places besides my own. She been teaching him for two years she says and what he has is a gift like she never seen before.

Gift I say. A gift is not like Cecil.

May I have the book she asks. I hand it to her. She opens it to a middle page. Like this listen to this. She begin to read to me from what apparently Cecil my son has written out. The name of it is "Soaring" and it is a string of words that say a bird is floating above the junkyard and has spotted a hot glowing old wreck below only the breeze sucks him down and he can't help but land in it. When she done reading the thing she look up at me like I should maybe be ridiculous with pleasure. I can't tell but that is my sense.

Is that the first chapter or what I want to know.

She lets out one of them whistly breaths that means I might overmatch her patience. These are poems of his life on the street she tells me. But they are brimful of accurate thoughts for all. Yet grounded in the tough streets of this area.

They have junkyards everywhere is my comeback to her.

But the bird Mister McCoy. The bird is soaring over death which is an old car wreck. The poet is wanting to be that white bird winging it free above death. What it really signifies is that Cecil want to be let off from having to die. That is the point of it she says.

Now to me this point is obvious but I feel sad for a second about Cecil. Two things he never going to be is a white bird.

Read on I suggest.

She slides out a smile for me that lets me know I'm catching on. Then she turn the book to another page. This was in some big-time poetry magazine she says. Then she read. The words of this one are about a situation I recognize. The poet has ripped off his momma's paycheck to pay back some bad dudes he ain't related to.

Hold it there I tell her. That is a poem that actually happen several times lady. Cecil a goddamn thief.

No no no. He wants to make amends for it. He wants to overcome the guilt of what he done.

I tell her it would be in the hundreds of dollars to do that. Is these poems going to get him that kind of

money? My question is beneath her. She won't answer it.

This poem has meanings for all the people she says.
They look into it and see their selves.

That is nice and interesting I tell her but how come
Wilma and me has to pay for this poem all alone? Everybody who looks in it and see their selves ought to pay
some back to us.

This comment of mine puts pressure on her cool and
she begins to pace about the room. The room is clean
enough but the furniture is ragged. I have a hip weakness
and janitor work pains it. Wilma has the job now.

The lady stops and looks out the window. Two cars
is blocking traffic to say what's going on to each other.
Horns are honking. People get hurt over things like that.

Mister McCoy do you love Cecil?

There was a time I answer. It was a love that any daddy
would have. But that was way back. If I love Cecil now it
is like the way I love the Korean conflict. Something terrible I have lived through.

He has changed Mister McCoy. He has got in touch
with his humanity. If he had a place to live he could be
paroled to start fresh.

I believe I will sit down. As I say it I drop to the three-
legged chair by the door. I am thinking of my son Cecil.
He was one of a whole set of kids Wilma and me filled out
because we had only each other. He ate from the same pot
of chili as the rest but he turned out different. His eyes

were shiny and his nose turned up instead of being flat. The better he knows you the more relaxed he is about stealing you blind. Same pot of chili but different.

I don't believe we want to take him back I say.

But you are his family. There is no one else for him.

Family yes but main victims too lady. I reach up and pull the bridge from my mouth which leaves a bad fence of my teeth showing. See that? I ask. Cecil did that. He wasn't but fifteen when he did that.

He has changed she says again. She says it like that settles it.

I don't believe it. He may well write out poems that say he sorry and guilty but I am leery of him. You listen to this lady. This porch right here. I was standing on this porch right here when it was less sunk and Cecil was out there in the street with a mess of boys. They were little but practicing to be dangerous someday. One of them picks up a stone and tosses it at the high-up streetlight there. He misses it by a house or two. He ain't close. I stood there on the porch out of curiosity and watched. They all flung stones at the light but none was close to shattering it. Then Cecil pick up a slice of brick and hardly aims but he smash that light to bits. As soon as it left his hand I seen that his aim for being bad was awful accurate.

Well she says. He seems sensitive to her.

Oh he can do that lady. He could do that years ago.

You are a hard nut she tells me. He is lost without you. His parole could be denied.

Tell me why do you care? I ask her this but my suspicion is she would like to give Cecil lessons in gaiety.

Because I admire his talent Mister McCoy. Cecil is a poet who is pissed off at the big things in this world and that give him a heat that happy poets got to stand back from.

You want us to take him home because he pissed off? That ain't no change.

Artistically she say wheezing that put-down breath again.

Lady that ain't enough I tell her. Let me show you the door.

When we are on the porch she wants to shake hands again but I don't chew my cabbage twice. I have been there so I lead her across the yard. Her cheeks get red. I look up and down the neighborhood and all the homes are like mine and Wilma's. The kind that if they were people they would cough a lot and spit up tangled stuff. Spit shit into the sink.

At her car she hands me the booklet. It is yours she says. Cecil insisted.

I take it in my hands. I say thank you.

She slips into the rattly old thing and starts the motor. A puff of oil smoke come out the back and there is a knocking sound.

I lean down to her window.

Look lady I say. Wish Cecil well but it is like this. He ain't getting no more poems off of us.

Her head nods and she flips her hand at me. The monster band-aid on the hood has caught my eye again. What kind of craziness is that about I wonder. I want to ask her but she shifts the car and pulls away. So I am left standing there alone to guess just what it is she believe that band-aid fix.

The Horse in Our History

The body fell within a shout of a house that still stands. A house shown up rudely in morning brightness, a dull small box gone shabby along the roof edge, with tar shingles hanging frayed over a gutter that has parted from the eaves and rolled under like a slackened lip. The yard between the house and the railroad tracks has become an undistinguished green, the old oaks have grown fatter with the decades, and new neighbors have built closer. At the bottom of the yard near the tracks there are burnished little stumps where elms that likely witnessed everything had been culled in the 1960s, probably, after the Dutch blight moved into our town and caught them all.

The body fell within a shout, and surely those in the house must have heard something. Shouts, pleas, cries, or brute laughter carrying loudly on that summer night before the war, here in the town this was then, of lulled hearts and wincing spirits, a democratic mess of abashed citizenry hard to rouse toward anything but winked eyes and tut-tuts on "negro matters." A Saturday in summer, the town square bunched with folks in for trading from the hills and hollers, hauling okra, tomatoes, chickens, goats, and alfalfa honey. Saturday crowds closed the streets around the square to traffic, and it became a huge veranda of massed amblers. Long hellos and nodded good-byes. Farmers in bib overalls with dirty seats, sporting dusted and crestfallen hats, raising pocket hankies already made stiff and angular with salt dried from sweat wiped during the hot wagon ride to town. In the shops and shade there were others, wearing creased town clothes, with the white hankies of gentlefolk folded to peak above breast pockets in a perfect suggestion of gentility and standing. The citizenry mingled—Howdy, Hello, Good gracious is that you? The hardware store was busy all day, and the bench seats outside became heavy with squatting men who spit brown splotches toward the gutter. Boys and girls hefted baskets of produce, ate penny candy, and screamed, begged nickels so they could catch the cowboy matinee at the Avenue Theater. Automobiles and trucks parked east of the square, wagons and mules rested north in the field below the stockyard pens. Toward evening the drinking and gambling men would gather to cheer or curse or wave weapons when local horses were raced on the flat, beaten track that circled the pens.

It was a man named Blue who fell on a night that followed such a day, a man and a falling I knew only from whispers, and the whispering had it that Blue tended horses here and there and was the only jockey around who could get the very best from a spectacular dun gelding named Greenvoe.

Mrs. E. H. Chambliss, in conversation outside Otto and Belle's Barbecue, probably in June of 1976: "That horse had a grandeur like no man and few beasts. He'd fly if he wanted to go slow."

Mr. Todd Pilkington, smoking in the men's room just before the funeral of a classmate he'd served beside at Anzio, spring 1984: "I've heard that horse mentioned—but wasn't that from you? Askin' me at some other funeral?"

Mr. Edward H. Chambliss, during a phone call in winter of 1994: "That nigra Blue was the best rider and hand hereabouts in them days, and him'n your granddaddy trained that horse up together real well. Real well."

My father, as the whistling breaths from his oxygen tubes kept the cat scared, and after the dog had smelled the near future on his master and run into the woods, never to return, the week of his death, 1993: "Son, I heard the water pump squeakin' in the yard late that night. That old pump, gushin' water for quite a spell, so late, and voices."

Black families had been recruited in Oxford, Mississippi, and brought to town by Dr. Brumleigh in 1910. The doctor owned vast fruit orchards just east of town, several hundred acres, and brought fourteen complete families north to work them for him. A bare clutch of rudimentary houses were built for the families on a gullied slope out of view from the square in the still largely forsaken northeastern reaches of town. The orchard failed within a decade. The blacks remained in homes that were soon too small, unsnug, and uneven against the sky. New rooms were made of what was easily found— wood scraps from backyards and trash piles, sheets of crumpled metal blown free by storms, chicken wire, river stones, with foundation stumps of almost the right size tipping the floors slightly this way and that. There were no romantic entryways or cozy embellishments. Windows cracked at angles as the houses relaxed further into the dirt.

Mr. Micah Kerr, beside Howl Creek, holding a cane pole while watching his bobber not bob, around 1969: "Them days, boy, furniture'd really start a-fallin' of a Saturday night over on Nigger Hill, there. Somebody'd a-get to fussin' with somebody else 'til furniture started flyin' and a-fallin', and that fussin'd go on and on 'til the makin' up started, which was usually louder."

My oldest living relative, who had, with great single-mindedness, remarried in less than a year, at her spacious new home, late 1993: "Don't write that. Why write that?

There wasn't any murder like that. It *never* happened. Never happened. And please listen good to me for once—they're not *all* dead yet."

The horse was, in most versions of the story, a bangtail grown powerful from running the sand bottoms of the Jacks Fork. Sometimes the horse had been stolen out of Sallisaw by one of the Grieve brothers, or a sly stranger who gave a false name on sale day and promptly left town. The horse was always dun, a bitter gelding, with a crisp stride and endless stamina. A horse worth fighting over.

Mr. Willie Johnstone, bourbon in hand, at a fish fry of redear perch on the Eleven Point, 1995: "I guess your granddaddy and ol' Blue was with the horse most days in them years. The lunch whistle'd blow at the mill'n lots of times you'd pretty quick see William Sidney walkin' the path yonder above Eccleston's, the path that's gone now but used to be the nigh cut through those woods that were there and came out into a backyard on the Hill. Fetchin' ol' Blue, I guess, to work that horse for the lunch hour in a field somewhere over there. I can still see him in my head, his shape goin' up that path—your granddaddy walked about like you do, kid, sort of hunched, like he was halfway duckin' from somethin' all the time."

Mrs. E. H. Chambliss, with her eyes closed and her hands clasped, on a porch swing in July 1995: "Oh, them two loved that horse. Which is sad, 'cause I think the horse is what killed him, really. The heartbreak, don't you know?"

Mr. Tom Finney, after my father's funeral, while carving a ham: "Shit, boy, his name wasn't Greenvoe—wherever'd you get that from? And he wasn't much of a horse, neither, if I'm rememberin' the horse you mean. Used to stop on the far half of the track and drop horse apples in the midst of a goddamn race—that sound like a great champ to you?"

Mr. Ronnie Thigpen, at his daughter's home near Egypt Grove, with the television blaring world news and a rack of medicine bottles on the table at his side, 1994: "There had been a drunk hobo run over by a train'n broken apart a month or so earlier, so when I seen all this blood'n splintered wood'n stuff, I thought, Uh-oh, another drunk hobo forgot to jump. Then I seen it was a nigger, a nigger from town, there, that had forgot to jump. So I told the man at the train depot there was a sort of familiar-lookin' nigger dead in the weeds over by the tracks, and I guess he flagged a deputy."

My oldest living relative, while picking cherries from her yard trees, 1996: "That's 'cause you got the name wrong. His name wasn't Blue—it was *Ballou*. Folks misheard his last name and thought it was his first name, so that's what he got called. His wife used to be around, did housework and the like, and her name was Ballou. Look for him under Ballou."

Summer had its fangs out sharp and long that year,

sucking the joy from every sunny hour. The heat led to erupting meannesses between intimates, bursts of spite that bubbled the truth up top to be hurled from one sweated sopping side of the bed to the other, never to be truly forgotten or gotten over. Howl Creek, a rumpled, dissolute puddling of water, became the nearest splashing place, and many folks of both sexes took small relief in the darkness there. A fainting quiet fell over the darkened town, and headaches ebbed in the silence, until an approaching train would release a rallying moan into the night. The railroad tracks ran beside the creek and the moan stirred sleep all across town.

Sheriff Solomon Combs, in a ledger found under a basement staircase at the courthouse, dated August 4, 1938: "Ballou. Colored. First name not sure. Drunk and hit by a train hauling timber. Deceased. Accident."

Mrs. E. H. Chambliss, waiting for hot rolls at the Ramada Inn buffet, on Easter Sunday, 1996: "The horse. I'm sure anything that might've happened, or maybe didn't, was about that horse."

Mr. Tom Finney, in the parking lot outside Kenny's Walleye Restaurant, summer 1996: "That worthless pony is probably still lollygaggin' on the far turn to spread horse apples, Danny. Hurry'n you can maybe still catch a glimpse of 'im yet, dawdling along the rail with his ass to the finish line and his tail in the air."

Someone official must've carried the news to the Hill. Knocking on doors to raised houses made of things not meant to be nailed together, but that stood for years, invalid structures patched further with odds and ends as passing seasons brought rot to the wood and old nails fell away. In the shade and fine dust beneath the houses, dogs have belly-dragged in and out until belly-shaped draws have been wiggled into the dirt. Kids follow dogs, and on the Sundays of most seasons muffled playing voices rise from the shaded crawl spaces and catch the wind to fly. Knock, knock—You Blue's wife? These li'l girls his kids? Well, he won't be home no more. Jumped in front of a timber train. Must've been drunk. You can bury the boy over at Sadie's.

Mr. Edward H. Chambliss, with his chin in the air and his ancient fists balled, on his front porch, early 1997: "William Sidney always was my best friend, goddamn you, Danny. And best friend don't mean nothin' if you won't stand for each other when the bad time comes. You might oughta keep clear of me. You might oughta do that. And don't call my wife, neither."

My oldest living relative, on the phone, early 1997: "These were not men lamed by any sorts of doubts about anything they did. Or *might do yet*—hear me?"

An uncle who'd had two ships blown wide and sunk beneath him in the Pacific, and came home with what they called "shell shock"—a cracked and occasionally cascading state of mind that was accompanied by a delicate lacing of public shame—on the phone from Australia, where he'd emigrated in 1955: "I knew Blue from when I ran errands for the men out at Cozy Grove, the bar there. I never saw him with a horse. He wasn't much higher'n a belt buckle, but he was stronger'n Limburger cheese. He'd carry feed sacks from town for a nickel. I never heard of Dad doin' much of anything with horses, neither, but go broke bettin' on 'em. You knew Dad was born well-to-do, didn't you? Had all that land once out by JJ Highway. Lost everything before I was born on moonshine and ladies in red and mighty slow horses, and never even said sorry, either."

So it's written down for an accident by the law, and the Ballou kids from that home-sawn house on the Hill come along fatherless into the war years, years that were hard on everybody, those wrinkling years of rubber rations, gas rations, meat rations, and unlimited worry, worry, every day the worry and the wrinkling and another supper leached from the same ham bone and more navy beans. See them waiting for dark before touring the square during the holiday season, heavy wet misting clouds between the tall lamps and their feet, pausing before the keenly garish shop windows, dampening scarves molding to their heads, wearing the uncertain slanting gaze of children who've been scalded other times for acting too familiar. A damp virtuosity of misshapen reflections on the street, the windows, the eyeglasses of the few walkers passing by, and two girls noting to each other the presents they most favored from shops they'd never go inside.

My father, drinking the whiskey he loved in the shadowed garage, with meddlers out of sight, fall 1992: "We each of us get dealt a lot of cards by our old ones, son, but you don't want to play them all."

The Hill as it was is vanished now, finished off by high heels and humiliated scolds, flattened to nothing and the scraps carted away in 1956. The sound of her high heels clicking on sidewalk cement brought water to the mouths of men within ear of her sashay, moist and listening as she came along so avid and fluid, with fluctuating mounds, the clicks entering their heads with the rhythm of dreams. A blooming of taffeta and a sweet woozy smell. Her voice was rich and round and rolled on and on, seducing with each spin, and the voice gave her a fresh name—Dyna Flo. A smitten car dealer used her in local radio spots, and she said the tagline so it held within it the promise of everything craved: "It's the Dyna Flo that makes it magic, folks. Come on out to Yount's Buick'n see for yourselves." Mr. Yount fell her way, his wallet held open and his mind helplessly made up. He swung by on Saturday nights with bottles of hooch and sporting friends, and the friends soon fell her way, too, and dripped dollar bills to her floor. Dyna Flo Ballou, her first name lost just as her father's had been, walked tall and flush and brought stray bits of finery to the Hill: curtains of bright yellow, brittle champagne glasses, expensive dresses from St. Louis in the wrong color for my skin, honey, that were soon worn by young girls mopping the floors of town.

My oldest living relative, during a warm winter, while her husband cleaned fish near Mammoth Spring: "She was drop-dead gorgeous. That gal got prettier every time I saw her, and she stopped traffic *the first time* I saw her. And, lordy, that voice—that Dyna Flo voice! No, no, she wasn't the kind of beauty you could ever miss—had eyes 'bout as blue as yours, Danny. We used to run into her sometimes when you were tiny. She always wanted to touch you. Touch your nose, tickle your cheek. Just touch you."

A schedule was arranged between the men with money, and Dyna Flo laughed low and golden from her porch steps until heard by wives who couldn't stand the sound nor the fact of her. The men were shamed but would not give her up, and marriages split in spots that never healed. Humiliated, the wives gathered uncles, brothers, friends from church with white robes and sticks, and during a rainy spell went to Dyna Flo's house, kicked the door aside, and threw everything she had into the yard-mud. Get out of town, tonight, or the same train'll hit you that hit your daddy. A week later every household on the Hill received a letter from the city, telling them to vacate the premises while water lines and sewers were put in and the streets were paved. We'll let you know when you can come back.

Mr. Tom Finney: "Most likely St. Louis. That's what I

heard. Folks was rough on colored people then, and black was the main one of them colors."

Mr. Ronnie Thigpen, Egypt Grove, 1994: "I went back by once the sheriff come along for a look. There was a bunch of two-by-fours that was splintered a little bit and had bloody places on 'em. Five or six, I guess. I seen the sheriff sort of kick those two-by-fours away from the tracks, down into the creek there. That's when he said, 'Looks to me like ol' Blue jumped in front of a timber train. Amen.'"

Mrs. E. H. Chambliss, accosted and held by the wrist, outside the Front Street Church of Christ in 1998, a month after her husband's death: "They was all brought together by love, Danny. The love of that horse. Your granddaddy doted on that thing, him'n Blue, then somethin' soured and Blue got drunk'n died. That horse was *magnificent*, hear? Beautiful to see, he was. Would've won any race he could've been got to—just that special. He was just so special."

My oldest living relative, sitting in a shaded parlor, upon reading my notes and turning over the last page, folded her old hands and closed her eyes: "There never was a horse. The rest is true."

Woe to Live On

I. Coleman Younger,
The Last Is Gone—1916

The river takes it from almost anywhere, trims branches with floating logs, smoothes edges on miles of rocky bottom and sandy bank, distorts the shape of the former tree by sucking it down at a hundred eddies of swirling murk, then spewing it back to the polishing touches of the everlasting current. Sometimes the river leaves the driftwood on a sandbar's lip, or jabbed into a dike—a present for me. I transport such gifts to my workshop. There I take my Barlow and ease it against the wood, scraping gently at the layers, taking substance

109

away to reduce the piece to the design I see in it. I labor on it for days, and I have been laboring thusly for years, but humility commands an admission—many times the river's hand carved more truly, and I bring no improvement.

On the day that I learned Coleman Younger had passed on to his stoked reward I searched for a special piece, and the river, now an occasional ally, sharing with me both muddy history and uncertain age, obliged.

I enlisted a hangdog grandson to assist me. His name was probably Karl, although he looked a lot like Kurt, especially as regards his subdued aspect. They are both like their father; blond-headed Dutch boys with that sort of Germanness that tape-measures all it meets and argues the logic of all that is not numbers. Not what I'd ever wanted to be, or been, or even tolerated.

The rarity of that clean-shaven oak length being so handy was not lost on me. Luck is a goddess, but if you bet on her she will desert you faster than a Frenchman. But that day I did not hope for luck, so there it was, a four-foot section of river-planed oak. There is never much oak, and this oak was on the first sand spit below the bend in the Missouri River. Karl or Kurt and I never had to wet a boot. We dragged a trail through the packed sand, he being too young to lift it alone and me too close to being young again, I feared. We lugged it along the path through the trees, up the glistening mudbank by the railroad tracks, then across the rails and back to town.

We pulled the wood onto our shoulders when we came to Main Street, me in the lead, my hunched form not much taller than the boy's. Our boots slipped on the cobblestones, from brick to brick, not slickly enough to trip us, but enough to lend a whoosh to our passing. There were louts on horseback, the shod animals sparking with each step, to avoid. Hemsath the egg man left his wagon in our path with one of his girlish brood sitting on the seat, using a switch to tease the mule about the eyes. A mule will not tolerate such levity long, so we stepped quick and put the pair behind us.

As we passed the Fremont Room of the Saint Charles Hotel, nearly home, a voice called out to me.

"Old Roedel," he said. "You must be sad that Younger has gone. You may be all that is left now." I turned to see who spoke. It was Harvey Ball, a man of two-shot killing size, as death would have to scream its presence a while to make it known to the ends of his form. "Let me buy you a drink."

"I am not a drinking man," I said. "You know this."

Ball had that confidence that horsey size gives a man. He reached out to grab my shoulder. "Naw. Come on now, Roedel. You must've split a jug with Black John Ambrose of an evening." I shook his hand off but he took no hints. "William C. Quantrill, the Jameses and Youngers, and Arch Clements and Pitt Mackeson—you tellin' me they were Baptist men? True Vine Pentecostal and would not drink?"

"I am telling you this—in many a jug there is a trigger, and where there are triggers, fingers multiply."

"You have plenty of fingers from the history of it," Ball said. "Did yours work dry?"

Karl or Kurt nudged me in the calf but did not speak. We began to walk on but Ball did not move from our path.

"I whip mules that buck me," I said. "Beware."

As we trekked on, Ball said something in a stingy voice that was to the point of, why hadn't his elders hanged me with the other bushwhackers, or cut me into finger candy like Arch Clements.

It is a good question, and I can put no answer to it.

We dropped the driftwood in the back room of the house. I did my sleeping in that room, as well as my carving. It was as near to being out of my son's house as I could be without sacrificing the benefits of stove heat.

My son, Jefferson, was in a stir over his evening paper. The donnybrook in Europe was of great importance, he said. The important wars are fought at home, among friends, I said. He said they will be killing Germans wholesale in this one, and didn't that please me? I am an American of sorts, I said. Germans are not my breed. You miss the point wide, he said.

My room safeguarded me from his ignorance. Behind the closed door I began to carve, I knew not what. Wood flakes curled about my feet and gathered on my clothes and hair. My knife turned in patterns I could not foresee, and something I did not expect would come of it. The worst and best in this life are that way.

Tea trays, I have made, and tankards with handles like an antelope's head, and hat racks and lazy Susans. But this night it was war and Coleman Younger and this land where Germans can change their names but not their ways that governed my blade by ghostly touch. It had been war enough for any man, less those blood-demons who choose man's form as disguise, and it was this I would show, if my hand be true, my blade honest in its cuts.

When hunger hailed me I dropped the knife and entered my son's house. Jefferson, Herta, and the boys were gathered in the main room, huddled beneath a tall glowing globe of light. Herta was reading aloud from Alcott, and the boys' rapt attention to such childishness insulted me. I remembered a time when their age would have had consequences, for they were mostly over twelve. I stood alone while they all sat. Soon Herta ceased reading. She began to look to Jefferson, he to her, the boys to me.

"You boys," I said, "have reached what we called the killing age."

Jefferson turned shocked, as if two and two had retreated into three, then mad. He stood and addressed me. "Your melancholy past is not meant for the ears of the young."

"No," I said. My feet carried me from the room, my son glaring at me. "You are wrong." He does not love me for he is German-proud, and believes that had time and history allowed for it, it could have been him as easily as another. He knows—and he is right. "No, it can be meant only for them. Only for them."

II. I Have Been Found in History Books

We rode across the hillocks and vales of Missouri, hiding in uniforms of Yankee blue. Our scouts were out left flank and right flank, while Pitt Mackeson and me formed the point. The night had been long and arduous, the horses were lathered to the withers, and dust was caking mud to our jackets. There had been whiskey through the night, and our breaths blasphemed the scent of early-morning spring. Blossoms began a cautious bloom on dogwood trees, and grass broke beneath hooves to impart rich, green odor. The Sni-A-Bar flowed to the west, a slight creek more than a river, but a comfort to tongues dried gamy and horses hard rode. We were making our way down the slope toward it, through a copse of hickory trees full of housewife squirrels gossiping at our passing, when we saw a wagon halted near the stream.

There was a man holding a hat for his hitched team to drink from, a woman, a girl in red flannel, and a boy who was splashing about at the water's edge, raising mud. The man's voice boomed to scold the boy for this as he had yet to drink.

"Dutchman," Mackeson said, then spit. "Goddamn lop-eared Saint Louis Dutchman." Mackeson was American and had no use for foreigners, and little for me. He had eyes that were not set level in a bent face, so that he saw you top and bottom in one glance. I watched him close in gunplay, and kept him to my front.

"Let us bring Black John up," I said.

I turned in my saddle and raised my right hand above me, waved a circle with it, then pointed ahead. Black John brought the boys up, he taking one column of blue to the right, Coleman Younger taking the other to the left.

The Dutchman heard the rumble of hooves but had no chance to escape us. We tightened our circle about the wagon, made certain the Dutchman was alone, then dismounted.

The family crusted around the Dutchman, not in fear, but to introduce themselves. Our uniforms were a relief to them, for they did not look closely at our mismatched trousers and our hats that had rebel locks trailing below them.

Most of the boys led their mounts to the stream, opened whiskey bottles, and generally tomfooled about near the water. Black John Ambrose, Mackeson, me, and a few others confronted the Dutchman. He offered his hand to Black John, whose stiff height, bristly black curls, and hard-set face made his leadership plain. Black John spit, as Americans are wont to do when confident of their might.

"Wilhelm Schnellenberger," the Dutchman said, his hand finally dropping back to his side.

I spit, then pawed the gob with my boot.

"Dutchman," Mackeson said. "Lop-eared Dutchman."

"Are you secesh?" Black John asked, his voice ever so coaxing. "Are you southern man?"

"No, no, no," the apple-headed Dutchman answered. His eyes wandered among us. He smiled. "No secesh. Union man."

The woman, the girl, and the boy nodded in agreement, the boy beginning to study our uniforms. Some of the fellows were kicking a stick to and fro, trying to keep it in the air, whiskey to the winner. It was a poetry moment: water, whiskey, no danger, a friendly sun in the sky, larks and laughter.

"Stretch his neck," Black John said. "And let's be sharp about it."

The woman had some American, and the Dutchman had enough anyway, for when she flung her arms about him wailing, he sunk to his knees. He was mumbling to his god, and I was thinking how his god must've missed the boat from Hamburg, for he was not near handy enough to be of use in this land.

"What's he babblin'?" Mackeson goaded me.

"He is praying to Abe Lincoln," I said.

Coleman Younger had a rope, but he would not lend it

as it was new, so we used mine. Mackeson formed it into a noose with seven coils rather than thirteen for he had no inclination to bring bad luck onto himself. Thirteen is proper, though, and some things ought to be done right. I raised this issue.

"You do it then, Dutchy," he said, tossing the seven-coiled rope to me. "Bad luck'll not change your course, anyhow."

As I worked to make the Dutchman's end a proper one, he began to talk to me. The situation had sunk in on the family and they had become dull. The Dutchman wiggle-waggled in that alien tongue. I acted put-upon by having thus to illustrate my skill in oddball dialects, lest I be watched for signs of pride in my parents' tongue.

"We care nothing for the war," the Dutchman said. I fitted the noose with thirteen coils around his neck. "We are for Utah Territory. Utah. This is not a war in Utah, we learn."

"This war is everywhere," I said.

"I am no negro stealer. I am barrel maker."

"You are Union."

"I am for Utah Territory."

Mackeson threw the rope over a cottonwood branch and tied it to the trunk. Some of the other boys hustled the Dutchman onto the seat of the wagon, startling the team and setting off screeches of metal on wood, mules, and women.

I stepped back from the wagon's path, then turned to Black John.

"He says he is not a Union man," I said. "He was codded by our costumes."

"Sure he says that," Mackeson said. "Dutchman don't mean fool."

"He does, does he?" Black John said. He was remounted and others were following suit. "Well, he should've hung by his convictions rather than live by the lie." Black John nodded to Mackeson. "He's a goddamn Dutchman anyhow, and I don't much care."

Mackeson slapped the mules on the rump and the Dutchman swung.

"One less Dutchman," Coleman Younger said.

They all watched me, as they always did, when wronghearted Dutchmen were converted by us. I mounted my bay slowly, elaborately cool about the affair.

The woman was grieved beyond utterance, the little girl whimpered behind her. The boy walked beneath his father's dancing boots, then made a move to loosen the rope about the cottonwood trunk. He was close to fourteen and still foreign to his toes.

I gave no warning but the cocking of my Navy Colt and booked the boy passage with his father. My face was profound, I hope, when I turned to Black John.

"Pups make hounds," I said. "And there are hounds enough."

Black John nodded, then solemnly said, "Jake Roedel, you are a rare Dutchman."

Mackeson looked at me as if I were something hogs had vomited.

"Did you see that?" he asked. "Shot the boy in the back! Couldn't shoot him face-to-face. Goddamn Dutchman! Why'd you shoot him from the back?"

"I am tender toward boys," I said. "But I would put a ball in your face, Mackeson, should affairs so dictate."

Black John then repeated himself on the sort of Dutchman I was, and we moved on to the silence of the family's pain. I positioned myself so that Pitt Mackeson's shoulder blades were ever visible to me.

Near dark, we shed our blue sheep's clothing. We were to rendezvous with Captain Quantrill west of Lone Jack, just above Blue Cut.

Camp was pitched and pickets put out while there was yet light to the day. Letters were written to homefolks by those that could, and rents in clothing were mended. Several of the boys, ever playful and game for fun, began to boot a ball of leather about the campsite, whiskey, as always, the victor's plunder.

I strolled about the camp whittling on a hickory branch that I had fated to be a water ladle. I watched the boys gambol on the grass but had not the spirit for games. I scooped the wood away, leaving a deep dish, intending this depth to aid in the settling of mud before drinking.

I squatted next to Coleman Younger, who had a bottle of whiskey that he had not won but that he intended to drink. He did not look my way when he handed the bottle to me. I dropped the ladle and sheathed my knife, then accepted the bottle. I appreciated his generosity to the measure of a quarter-pint on the first swallow.

"Do not think you are a good man," Coleman Younger said. "The thought will spoil you."

"I am a southern man," I said. "And that is as good as any man that lived 'til he died."

Coleman Younger was reddish in skin and hair with the temperament that is wed to that hue, and girth and grit enough to back it up.

"You are a southern man—that is proven," Coleman Younger said. "But a rare one."

For Coleman Younger to speak of me so set a glow in me that whiskey could not match, nor doubt extinguish. It was for this that I searched, communion and levelness with people who were not mine by birth, but mine by the taking. We drank into the dark, then slept, our bedrolls but a rifle's length apart.

In the night Captain Quantrill and his party had hallooed our pickets, then rode in and joined us. In the morning there was much cutting up as old comrades were reunited over salt pork and oat cakes. The James brothers from Clay County, Buck and Dingus as they were then known, frolicked with Coleman Younger, Arch Clements, and Black John. Captain Quantrill stood apart, his eyes flat beneath sleepy hoods, and his tongue wiping his lips like a frog sensing flies.

They had taken ten prisoners from the Union Home

Guard at Waverly. General Ewing, the leader of the Union occupation scum for the entire district, had issued an order concerning rebels as a mass, and our sort in special, that said if caught we were to be tried and hanged, or shot, whichever took less trouble. This led to some debate among us as to what we should do with the Yankees now in our possession. There were a few among the prisoners known personally to some of us from before the hostilities. There was a sunken-chested, half-sized one among them I knew as Alf Bowden, who hailed from my town. I had once helped him raise a barn on a summer day and danced with his sister 'til her face flushed and we both sweated, but I was not in his debt, nor he in mine. It was a good war for settling debts—some were settled before they were incurred, no doubt—but thin-skinned fairness rarely crabbed youthful aim. Alf said hello to me and I to him, but the courtesy of that situation required no more than that, so there we left it. It would be sad to see him killed, but sadness was on the flourish in those times.

There was no rain on the wind, only the smell of thawed mud and early blossoms, but the boys were lazied by the previous days, so we made a carnival of the camp and sought no demonstrations with our enemy. The ball of leather was trotted out, with nearly the whole of both parties joining in on the sport, stomping the mud into a glue that sucked down boots and held them there. The whiskey was running low and this raised tempers. Riley Crawford, not yet sixteen but the deadest shot among us, missed the ball with a kick of vigor and shinned Big Bob Flannery. Big Bob knotted him one on the head, and Riley cut him under the armpit by reflex. Captain Quantrill then snatched up the ball and hid it away, saying he would shoot any of us who murdered a comrade.

After the noon meal, Captain Quantrill and Black John announced that there would be haircuts for all, because we were to be disguised as Yankees once more for a ride into the Union district around Lexington, and our rebel locks would be noticed. There was much grumbling about this, for our locks were of the southern style and our pride and banner. "I'd rather robe myself with dog skins," Big Bob Flannery said. "For if we must look like Yankees to win, we will be defeated in victory." The bulk of us saw the sense in the notion, however, and went along with it, shaving and cutting our hair as if spiffying up for a church dance, but Big Bob had to be held down while Arch Clements harvested his hair patch. Little Arch being that close to his scalp with a Bowie knife sobered Big Bob, for he, like all of us, had witnessed the fashion in which Arch barbered dead, and practically dead, Yankees.

After that Coleman Younger, Little Arch, Pitt Mackeson, and me sat under the husky tree that the prisoners were roped to. Captain Quantrill had made a present to Coleman Younger of a new Enfield rifle that had been captured. We admired the weapon and made chat about its supposed power, the prisoners joining in with a remark here and there.

Pitt Mackeson tried to flare me by mentioning in a bad mouth the incident with the Dutch boy.

"If the boy had freed the rope the hanging would've been scotched and required doing over," I said.

"Judas worked quick, too," said Pitt Mackeson.

Coleman Younger stroked the Enfield and chambered a round. "You did right," he said. "Dead from the front is no more dead than from the back. It is a question of opportunity."

"So is chicken stealing," Mackeson said.

My arms ached already from the thought of digging his new home, for I was thinking he would soon be in it. "Jake did right."

Arch Clements untied the prisoners and told them to stand, then retied them in a file of sorts. "Stay in your line, soldier boys," he said in his squeaky voice. "For we shall march your meals down."

Coleman Younger placed his hand on top of my head as he stood. "It was nothing," he said, "but right." He ran his hand along the smooth stock of the Enfield, then raised it to his shoulder. He sighted into the belly of the prisoner at the head of the column.

"Leave off with the jokes," the prisoner said.

The Enfield fired and the first three Yankees tumbled.

Coleman Younger chambered another round. "I would've thought more," he said. "So far this ain't special."

The rest of the camp was dropping letters, gun rags, needles, tin cups, and favored corncobs to watch. I thought Captain Quantrill might be peeved by this employment of his prisoners, but he made no move to halt it.

The next shot felled only two, and not cleanly. Their moans sounded like man and wife in a feather bed.

Coleman Younger chambered another round.

"Not exactly a Sharps, is it?" he said.

Little Arch made a straight line of the Yankees again as they had drifted some. Alf Bowden was among the standing, and he called my name, which it must've hurt him to do.

"Let us save one," I said. I pulled Alf Bowden from the line, he being so limp he fell at my touch. "We can send him back to General Ewing, maybe, as a witness that his new law will cut both ways."

There was blood in the air. It drifted over my bare hands, spotting them like some rare mist. Alf Bowden was yet on his knees, his hands clutching at my legs, pulling himself toward me. The rare mist had freckled one of his cheeks, and his hair had been touched up at the ends by the same breeze, giving him a vaguely pheasant aspect.

The man and wife in the feather bed slept now, and the silence was glass, poised for the shatter.

"We all had friends," Coleman Younger said. He chambered another round. He was staring at me more thoughtfully than I found comfortable. "That is all off now."

"There is something to be gained by this sparing," I

said. I did not believe what I had said, but I said it, and hoped only to utter more dream-babble that would justify it.

"I yearn to hear about it," Coleman Younger said.

I was losing a comrade, this I could see. I had no retort.

A murderer of slyer instincts saved me and made of me a hero. Captain Quantrill had cozied up to us as we were engaged. He held a palm toward Coleman Younger, Little Arch, and Pitt Mackeson, who was fiddling with something near his holster. He then fixed me with a reverent gaze, an approving light coming to his eyes.

Alf Bowden babbled into my toes, his arms encircling my boots, his face between them.

"I quite see it," Captain Quantrill said. "Yes. We shall send him over to Sigel's brigade of Dutchmen near Warrensburg." Captain Quantrill worked his hands together as if to wash them. His feet were moving in little hops, and he would surely have danced had there been a suitable partner handy. "Oh, yes. They far outnumber us. They will want to make quick time and to do that they will come through Creve Coeur Gap. Oh, my, yes."

His plan could not be missed. Creve Coeur Gap was a narrow slit between two long bluffs that flanked the Blackwater River. General Franz Sigel, alerted by the winner from my mistake, and our most hated enemy, would seek the shortest route to our destruction—through the tall bluffs, thick timber, and slender passage afforded by Creve Coeur Gap.

125

"Just so," I said.

Coleman Younger and the others began to nod, then smile at me, their lips raising only on one side of their mouths.

"Jake Roedel," Coleman Younger said. "You are brilliant with mercy."

I had not foreseen this plan, but I was giving thanks for its arrival on more than one score. It had saved me my comrades and blessed me with an opportunity named Franz Sigel. He was called a general, and to Yankees and Dutchmen he was so. His very name herded furies into my heart. In my father's household he had been a saint, or near enough to it to have his picture above the mantel. He drummed up Dutchmen from among those foreigners who had come to America wanting to remain so. He oppressed me, and I longed to sight in on him. I had seen him lure them on, making himself a patriarch for those who would not mix, leading them to Fit Mit Sigel. Oh, the battles my father and I had on Sigel's account. We raged in his language, my face puffing, and his blue stubborn eyes glowing beneath his thick Prussian brows. He will keep you foreign, I said, and make you snobs about it. Is this wrong? was his reply. We never agreed; I chose to side with Americans and lost entry to the house that raised me.

I led Alf Bowden to a stew pot and fed him.

The brilliance of mercy being a thing that requires judicious use, the other Yankees died. Two shots.

When Alf Bowden could once more keep his feet beneath himself, we set him off on foot toward Sigel's brigade. It was over twenty miles, and he could not arrive there before dawn.

Around the campfires that night we cleaned our pistols, as we carried from four to eight apiece, the many shots the handguns afforded us over rifles being our chief asset, and the ace that allowed our small group to gamble with much larger ones.

There was considerable youth still in us, as by age that is what we were, and this, we felt, would carry the field. Setbacks had come our way, but cheerful, straight-backed desire to trade shots and victories wiped those from our minds.

There was much to look forward to that night as we oiled barrels and checked powder levels.

As I finished my hickory deep-dish water ladle, I listened to the men. Idle chatter about Coleman Younger's parole procedures dominated. Many speculated about the impulse for his actions, as he was not regularly cruel. What were his motives when he sighted that Enfield on the Union file, voices wondered, then squeezed the trigger? There were answers. Some seemed to suspect the scientific impulse, but I, I thought the priestly. He was gracing me for the Dutch boy. I could not rest with that in mind.

Before dawn we had reached Creve Coeur Gap and rendered the lush greenery and sweet earth bluffs into a slaughterhouse.. We perched on the ridges, then spaced ourselves down the far slopes, making a vee that promised clear shooting for all.

The sun was not yet straight in the sky when our scouts alerted us that troops were approaching. Captain Quantrill was devilish with his logic, for the Yankee-Dutchmen galloped headlong into our surprise. I searched the blue ranks for Alf Bowden but did not see him. My position was such that General Sigel was beyond my range.

The Yankees came on. We waited for the signal from Black John or Captain Quantrill, and I knew that I was among comrades now, for they had put their lives at stake over a plan they believed to be of my design.

I had spared one man and profited with a massacre of Dutchmen.

The signal was given.

I became famous for this.

III. Only for Them

I have died more times than one—perhaps three. This is not rare, but it may serve to stump the windiest of preachers, and a wandering eulogy is suited to those whose journey is uncertain in destination. I have no need for preachers, or faith in their selected destinations, but there must be a place, and I will not be misdirected.

I carved my own passport to that place; it will be as good as any.

Through the night I whittled, lessening, lessening, ever taking away from the oak. Reduction is the design I crave. My blade was a voice with a mind all its own, and it spoke to the wood in slashes, nicks, and great gouges. Flame from the kerosene lamp dodged about with the draft from the window, casting shadows where light had been, and light about my work. The pale wood chips gathered at my feet, a tribute to the diligence of my thick-veined hands and famous fingers.

When the cock had cried, then hushed before the grim, steel light of a rainy day, Jefferson opened my door. He wore high boots of the sort that are meant for polish and not for mud, and a suit of keen correctness, right down to the stiff boiled collar and the four-in-hand knot about his throat. His mustache was pruned so thin that it could be mistaken for a bonus lip.

"There are some things, Jacob," he said, "that I will not have in this house."

I felt no obligation to respond. Jefferson waddled across the room a bit, wishing I'd be provocative and force him into courage, but I was mild. He played with his watch chain, looping it through his fingers, waiting. There was some part of him that feared me, that was uncertain that I knew the boundaries of blood. It made us eerie together.

"Do not raise yourself into some sort of hero with my

children," Jefferson said. "Boys tend to admire war and lengthened necks and all. I know better and someday so shall they."

"I fought," I said, "for my comrades, and myself, but no more bravely than others."

"Your bravery," he said, nearly spitting it, "is a midnight legend." Jefferson leaned toward me, blowing his chest expansive and crossing his arms, as if I could be frightened. "So bold and brave were you that you managed to kill your father—too bad he failed to see the safety in being your traitorous comrade."

"I did not kill him."

"You did not pull the trigger."

"Exactly."

"Alf Bowden pulled the trigger," Jefferson said. "The one man you should have killed, you let go. Did you fail to realize that an American would seek satisfaction from your kin?"

Yes, I thought, gray heads had suffered while young ones went unnoosed. Alf Bowden was yielded to life while nine of his comrades were forfeited, but this did not make a friend of him.

"Shot him in the neck," Jefferson said. "In front of your mother, he not even having English enough to know why he was killed. Small blessing." Jefferson kicked about in the wood curls. "What a mess you have made." I said nothing. "Your scarlet oaf of a comrade, Younger, ruined you for me, Jacob. He should never have visited."

It was true; I lost something when Coleman Younger happened by. It was the year of the World's Fair in St. Louis, and he was not long out of prison. I had not seen him since I returned from Old Mex in sixty-eight, but I had read about him often. He came to the door and knocked. When I answered it he said, "Jake Roedel, it is your old comrade, Coleman Younger." I saw that he told the truth and said so, then welcomed him in. Prison had paled him, and he had become a pinkish man, a color I had never thought him capable of. I remembered him red. I offered him wine, but he was prepared with a flask of his own. We gathered at the table. Jefferson, a young man meeting history, sat at Coleman Younger's elbow. We drank. The freeness of my own remembrances encouraged my guest to candor, and he spoke truly of our shared activities. Jefferson questioned him, and he answered directly, not noticing that my son was of the generation that cared less for America than they did the land that earlier generations had fled. There was now pride about the awkward consonants of foreign names, and narcissism in noodles called spaetzle, and in porkpie hats called homburgs. In Coleman Younger's answers were accounts of the days of the Dutch boy, Alf Bowden, Creve Coeur Gap, and numberless others, for the war went on unblunted by my famous deed. Jefferson's eyes fixed on me when the talk shifted to baseball and the World's Fair, then he quietly left the house, easing the door closed behind himself. I knew then that he was lost to me.

"I could not turn him away," I said. "You gained from him—a great bitterness to drive you."

"My boys will not inherit such from me," Jefferson said. "They will not find that I killed my own people in the service of traitors, or that I scalped possible cousins for sport."

They littered Creve Coeur Gap. Their uniforms were valuable plunder, and their sourdough bodies began to rise with the sun. Little Arch Clements started it. They all watched me, and I knew it. They came off with a steady pull, a sound like that of a toothless grandma sucking on a cob of corn accompanying them. I saved mine for some time before flinging it to the river.

"I took no pleasure in that," I said.

"I take no pleasure in you," my son said.

He left me to myself.

I went back to work. The voice in my blade called out chop! chop! And my hand obeyed. Slash! Stab! The wood flew until only nubbins survived, and these I ground beneath my boots.

My hand had carved I knew not what, I had not restrained it, and what it wrought was bark chips and wood curls, sawdust and splinters.

Could this be? Could my passport be such?

The chips and curls would not mend. No other design would grow from them. I gathered a handful of the fragrant flakes and raised them to my face. My nostrils rested on the little pile, my tongue touched their salt.

Nothing but wood chips—the large rendered small, and confusing.

I blew on them and they began to spray about, then I tossed them to the corners.

Oh, that voice in my blade had divined me well. I would seek no other monument.

Dream Spot

It's always a mess when they want to trumpet their love, say the words that make it all clear and everlasting, announce that a hard bond has formed between them that will never break, snap, melt, never, then want Dalrymple to come up with some retort that proves it back. He had to guess. He never did quite feel it, but gave a try at thinking his way into love, love with her, the one sitting close, imagining himself deep inside her spirit, toward the very bottom, where it's fearful and wet and her secret hopes splash about. But the light goes out on that picture before he can find any feelings of his own down in all that black wet, and he's got to say something.

Just tell me what you want to hear.

Well, that sure ain't it.

How about trout?

I get carsick on that road—you know that.

I like how they let you catch them there first. Plus it's a pretty spot.

You can't say you love me, can you?

I think it all the time.

You just can't say it.

Aw, Janet, I love, love, love you! Love, love, love.

That's it, add insult, mockery. It's a weak man can't say love.

She's put her finger right on the button about him, which is embarrassing. It's so general, his problem, so everywhere among men, that he wants to add a wrinkle to it, some invented misery that makes it seem like he at least had a special sort of problem with love that was all his own. But what on earth would that be? That he was raised by foreigners who spoke a different language that had lots and lots of words but none of them were love? Or he can't reach his emotions good since his tragic baby went down with the ship or was lost in the fire or whatever? But he doesn't have any such excuse to give as an answer and instead opens another beer, looks out the window at the foggy hollows and damp dark bark, the vast forest of trees stripping down for the winter snooze.

The road is skinny and curvy, with no shoulder and deep gullies alongside, and plenty of people die alone in those severe gullies, impaled, twisted awry in their bones, bleeding out in slow drips, wondering why none of the kids in back is making a sound. Miss a curve, fly downward, see you in a day or two, my friend, maybe not so quick. Janet is snug against her window, eyes closed to slow the carsick welling in her chest. She's itty-bitty and wears glasses of the type ancient ladies favor, with little swan wings on the frame, stems hooked to a silver chain. Her hair is penny colored and lies down in a wide flat noodle that sticks to her forehead, a style she found while watching a sinister late movie in black-and-white that kept Dalrymple guessing just which sharpie actually had the bag of money to the very end. Her look makes her seem like a lady he should've met in some other life, one when there was more horn music, not so much this one. She's searched out clothes that go with her look, and this dress is crinkled black stuff with veil material across the high part of her chest and partway down the arms. Her shoulder blades are pale, the bone sharp and pressing on her skin, and she keeps a filterless cigarette burning between her fingers, raises each one and slowly adds bright red lipstick circles to the paper, red circles smooched at the same place every time. She does not inhale, but waves the butt about near the window like she's erasing the visible world with smoke as they motor along the blacktop.

There's suddenly a person ahead, hunkered at the edge of the road with a knapsack laid down, wearing a long green army coat and a knit cap pulled over the ears. The situation is so obvious the hitcher doesn't bother to throw a thumb out, just stares at the car, the stare suggesting the occupants should do the right thing by their fellow man, their fellow bum, their fellow teenage runaway.

Stop, Janet said. Stop—that's a woman. A woman in green, adrift and alone, way out here in the woods and mist.

Dalrymple always enjoyed the way Janet said things when she was off her meds. Her words then put special color to events, events he usually witnessed but hadn't noted any special color or significance to until she retold the event a minute after it happened. She'd built him a bunch of favorite memories that way. He'd hate to lose her.

What kind of woman is that?

She's lookin' like a man out here, so men passin' won't snatch her up and keep her chained in the basement.

You sure got a bad thing about men.

I got a bad thing about everybody if you pay attention.

Thirty yards past the woman Dalrymple stopped the car. He and Janet turned to look backwards over their seats, out the rear window. They watched the hitchhiker, who watched them in return. The hitcher bent to sit the knapsack upright, expecting to heft it to her back soon, run toward the car, say how ya doin', ask where they were heading. Janet stared hard, waving smoke from her view.

She craves you.

She what?

Craves you.

That's a great word. I guess I always have done that myself, crave stuff.

The hitcher walked in tight circles around the knapsack. She undid her long coat and held it parted with her hands on her waist. She wore an old sweater that must've been looser on her once, and green pants with lots of places to keep small things handy.

Janet threw a butt from the window, lit another. Her eyes were tightening behind those eyeglasses.

You are why she's here, my love. You. She's been looking for you all along without knowing it. She knew she was looking, just not that she was looking for you, and you alone.

Can she even see me from there?

She'll realize she has found you without knowing she'd wanted to after you back up for her and stop and she sees your face—where will that leave me?

Did you bring any pills at all?

She's a hundred percent gal under that coat, and you like new ones best of any.

(The funk of their lives sometimes wilted Dalrymple, made his vision shrink, this funk mostly the result of having punted earthly ambition, trimmed the wants from life, accepting a kind of decay, a rotted reduction of who they'd been capable of becoming at the start. He and Janet didn't mesh that well, always having petty dramas spring to life around them, but they couldn't decide to part, either, or make most simple decisions at all. Where to live, what to eat today, tonight, tomorrow, when to get out of bed, when to get out of bed again, which toothbrush, which channel, which bills to pay—all decisions they couldn't seem to make. Things just happened without selection or consensus. Even when they tried to pick dream vacations, a present to themselves, an exercise that ought to be purely sweet and silky smooth, they ended up frustrated with each other, devastated, really, by their inability as a couple to clearly prefer one dream spot over another— the Rockies?

My nose gets dry up there, bleeds on my pillow at night.

Texas?

I hate their costumes.

Los Angeles?

Sure, I'll hold the gun while you do the driving.

Ireland?

We can drink at home.)

Christ, Janet, it's been almost five years. I have been with you almost five years.

Almost five years coming to an end, judging by her eyes, such power in them, black, I think, with the future in there already up and walking around holding hands. She's just about got the details for you and her all worked out. I expect you'll live in Taos or one of those other places full of the holy heebie-jeebies, where crystals and chanting and such shit hold sway.

I'm not moving to Taos. I'm not learning a bunch of fucking chants. I don't get dazzled by shiny fucking rocks.

She does. She does. You don't have to like something if she does.

That sounds familiar.

The hitcher has bent and lifted the knapsack. She is watching the car from an angle, her face turned to the side, and there is a force about her, something sort of rumbling from her expression. She starts walking toward the car, sure of herself.

I can see it in her eyes!

She looks kind of cold, that's all.

Ready already to betray me. Didn't take long. She's got her hooks in you good.

There's no hooks.

Just exactly what you'd say if there were hooks in you good and deep.

Dalrymple shifted to reverse, removed his foot from the brake and floored the car toward the hitcher. She stood still, expecting him to stop, and as he neared she still expected him to stop, then she quit expecting him to stop and dove off the road and he swerved to hit her and missed. The car slid down the slope of the gully upright at first, arms inside raising to brace against the dash, the car slipping sideways, then picked up speed and rolled over, crushing saplings and shrubs, scrub oak and brambles, rolled twice more before slamming into a hickory tree. The wheels were in the air, spinning, all glass shattered, and the roof had lowered. Bone cracked in the meat of Dalrymple's arm and made a reddening hump in his shirtsleeve. Both knees hurt and he couldn't see well through the warm ooze, but he did see an arm wearing an overcoat come through the passenger window, move Janet's head aside, and reach beneath it for her purse. The hitcher came around to his side, then, and pushed on him and poked among his many pains until she could reach his wallet. She smelled of woodsmoke and spilled soup but didn't say anything, only grunted, then scrambled back uphill suddenly talking very happily in rhyme to somebody not present.

Janet was crumpled, mumbling, mushed badly inside her middle area. The skin was split on her forehead; her nose gurgled. Dalrymple and Janet hung upside down, hidden from the road and doomed together. Her face was topsy-turvy, lips torn and bleeding, moving weakly in the mess, slowly taking a shape that might've been a smile.

One United

The stories from my sleep bled into my morning chores and I kept trying to reclaim different ones, go back inside them, but they were slippery, hard to hold or even locate again. I had appeared in three or four movies over the night, and in daylight I hoped the better flicks might meld into one united story I could follow easy, live among for the day, but they couldn't quite do it. All morning I felt uncertain as to where I was in this flesh, at this time, and just how is it I got here, or got over the ocean if that's where I actually am. There was a shiny boy with yellow hair pedaling a bicycle, wearing wooden little shoes and britches that stopped under his knees, riding on fat tires in a foreign land of waving grain, but not one where bombs were dropping. Seems like he was in the one at the beach, too, when the nuns cleaning fish with pocket combs sang to Sleepy and me and Momma with her neck opened sideways while we floated toward the sun to burn away our faces. I had a paintbrush in hand, laying red over the walls already splashed that way in the movie that so often breaks into the middle of the others, takes over any of them, a movie of red, red, red I'd had explained to me so many times in group without getting it all the way ever. But then there he is still pedaling with a goose in the handlebar basket, his yellow hair boiling hard and making bubbles as he passes, and he knows me from someplace secret I don't remember ever being and smiles lopsided and mysterious my way.

Wait!

In the dull dutiful movie that had morning chores in it I walked the pasture bringing feed to the cows, kicking dewdrops into flash splinters, but feeling like large parts of me were yet inside those other shows, chasing that bicycle toward mountains I couldn't name and avoiding walls of redness and that smell. My thoughts chased after scenes occurring all over the world, scenes that fled faster than I could chase, and I sat on the grass feeling bereft, abandoned by my good dreams, surrounded by the others.

I reached about all over my memory for those better stories but couldn't get a grip.

The cows had chewed their fill and started to scatter when Sleepy came driving south, down the meadow from the hay barn to the north, straight through the pasture, over humped ground and old fallen branches. Tools and various metal bits bucked in the truck bed and clanged until he halted beside me. Sleepy terrified everybody around for certain reasons but me, who knew him in a different way: the day in the kitchen with that shape spreading red on the floor he said kind of soft to me, "Drop a hammer or somethin' in all that mess beside her, darlin', and maybe they'll think…" On this regular, slower day he hung his head from the window, a smoke pinched in his fingers, and said, "Run up and fix your hair, Rebecca. Run up and drag a brush through there, and put on a new polka-dot dress, why not? Somethin' that looks decent to people."

"Decent?"

"Now you're well again I kind of want you standin' behind me today. I want you with me."

"New polka-dots?"

"There's a dress in your closet now I left there for you."

"I have to recognize my choices plainly and be honest and know that I always have choices before…"

"There's only one dotted one."

Sleepy's eyes look like he's napping all the time. It's easy to think he's drowsing even when he looks straight at you, as his eyelids have been lame and droopy since he was born missing a needed muscle or something, so they don't ever open wide or shut tight. When he blinks there's a tiny rounded twitch over the eyeballs, but no real flapping of the lids. He's got various rough habits and rattler eyes, and his air of menace is sincere and fetching to certain sorts. There have been plenty of road-house gals who swooned for him, surrendered to his complete scariness, but none he kept long. Some gals went away of a sudden at night and left behind every-thing they owned that wasn't on them. Abandoned undies might flap from our clothesline for weeks.

The polka-dots belonged around me and had forever, it seemed, once I'd gone among them. I had too many shoes from all ages on the floor, shoes and boots for school and church or chores, and almost failed to maintain my com-posure properly from the buzzing confusion and doubt of choice they raised in my head, those dusty toes, stiff laces, childish sizes that didn't belong to me anymore—too much footwear and no clarity! clarity!—but finally I selected the white sneakers I already had on that they give out while you're in there and I'm used to feeling on my feet. The skirt flounced real twisty and shook those dots fizzy when I walked to the truck. Sleepy sped out the driveway and onto the blacktop, tromping the gas to-ward China Church, or maybe Dorta. His booze bottle slid underfoot on the turns until I dropped a sneaker on the neck. Out the window there's a blur of trees and fence posts, crows on wires and ponds scummed green, two kids racing three-wheelers over a puckered dirt mound.

"You got trouble?"

"Not for long."

I could hear inside his mind better now, too, since my return, the roundelay of sounds amok in the head—swift ripping sounds, human whimpers behind the door, that distant banjo striking notes curved so sharp only one ear can hear them and the other gets suspicious. I hoped not to ever again submit to the demands of such sounds, but I don't make that kind of promise to myself anymore.

Sleepy says, "You know any Wallaces?"

"From where?"

"From over toward West Table, on the Dorta road. Those ones."

"In school there were some, from by Bawbee, that dairy."

"These ain't related to those."

"Their cheese hardly melts."

"That's not the ones I mean."

"I don't, then."

"Good. That'll make it easy on you if they act up silly and start a fight."

Staff at the gate told me my life is all day-by-day from here on out.

At a certain spot he backed the truck a few feet onto a gravel road running to the head of a thin trail that led into the public forest, around Sulphur Ridge, then dropped to the Twin Forks River. On private land across the blacktop and down in a swale there was a nice red barn, well-kept and big, beside a huge pen of hogs dusting their skin in the sunshine. Up the slope beyond sat a white house of beaming windows, with fancy railings edging the porch, gray double doors to the root cellar slanted against the near wall, a swing chair on hair ropes hanging from a stooped tree in the yard. Past the house there stretched a long field of bright, gangly corn, then there was a scant line of trees, and behind them another field of a different crop that hadn't done much sprouting yet.

Sleepy said, "Ol' boy's got him some fat acres, don't he?"

"Good dirt."

"That means plenty."

Sleepy slouched in his seat and watched the house across the road, smoking cigarettes and punching the radio dial all over the place, seeking tunes he liked but finally giving up. In the quiet you could hear car tires sing low notes on the hard road while nearby birds tried to thwart the song with quick little trills. A burly beer truck passed, grunting slow toward Mountain View, the side painted with a tall picture of beer in a glass, beaded and beckoning, and Sleepy chuckled, then said, "Whatta you think?"

"I must abstain from alcohol and other stimulants."

"They haul 'em warm, anyhow."

We sat there until the sun was announcing the lunch hour in the sky, and from behind us there came a sound on the gravel, a sweet crunching, two boys on bicycles, both in blue jeans and T-shirts of several colors wrung together, sweating brightly. Wide hats hid their hair, big shades hid their eyes. They rolled to the pavement, looked up and down the blacktop like they were waiting on someone coming to get them, then turned their bikes about and pedaled back to the trailhead. Their feet were clamped to the pedals, and the bikes were the kind meant for mountainsides and rock creek beds. Both boys nodded at the truck, and one wore a nice necklace featuring a circled silver thing that sent the sun rays back at me spinning.

Sleepy said, "Oh, my—look at them wheels. That kind costs plenty. "

"Is that one's hair yellow?"

"Them boys look like they'd be easy—but there's the man now, going up to the house for his eats."

"Those hats hid the colors."

"I won't show my gun 'til they show theirs."

The lane in is narrow, with separated wheel ruts coated by white chat and a taller mohawk of grass between. Every passing tire spreads the chat a bit more and deepens the ruts likewise. The farmer steps onto the porch as Sleepy drives near. Through the screen door I can see a woman of wife age, and a grown son in shadow behind the screen. Sleepy and the farmer lock eyes a minute with the engine running, then Sleepy turns the key. He says, "Stand in the yard, there, and look decent unless I call you over."

"I have been instructed and will comply."

I take my stand by the tailgate and wait. Chickens range about the yard, flapping and pecking, murmuring to each other, the kind with red leggings and sharp clucks. Sleepy and the farmer meet on the porch, and the wife steps out while the son lingers on the other side of the door to be nearer the shotgun rack, I imagine. That swing chair on hair ropes is just for show, it seems, and couldn't hold much weight, the hair being loose and rotted, ready to snap. The wife is a pretty lady but doesn't look too good just now—pale, hands at her sides, like she's expecting to see her world flipped wrong way up and dropped on its head at any instant now. Her lipstick is perfect even on lips shaking that way. The farmer is trying to speak back, but pretty soon he stops and Sleepy leans close to him and keeps talking. Young corn smell is coming strong across the yard, with the smell of turned dirt, and chickens. That son opens the door and stands in the way of it closing.

He's the shiny boy my sleep sent to me. Yellow hair is quite clearly boiling bubbles on his head.

Sleepy laughs alone, the only laugher on the porch. I can hear him say in slowed words, plain and loud, like talking to a kid, "Now, Edward, you've known me most all my life—you know damn well that wasn't me you seen."

You have to believe your dreams keep your best interests in mind and wouldn't send anybody wrong to you.

I went without thinking or making the choice over the grass to the steps, the way my sleep would want, and swung my dots, sliding past the wife and the farmer. The boy looks at me like he doesn't remember bicycling through fields of waving grain all night so clear as I do.

"I'm here about your yellow hair."

"I'm listenin' to what they say."

"Don't you have wooden shoes you wear sometimes?"

"I know who you are."

I start to reach for his hand, to hold it and feel the warm fingers, and splash the other hand up to his head of boiling yellow and pop those hot bubbles with my fingertips, gather the bubbles and pop, pop, pop but you can startle dreams with sudden changes and they lose their shape and drain through the cracks to somewhere you can't find, so I don't. "Maybe you only wear them for going out bicycling?"

"You need to get off this porch."

Sleepy clomps down the steps and into the yard, suddenly stops, goes on high alert, raises his nose, and takes several big sniffs of the air. "Is that your barn burnin'?"

The farmer, the wife, the son, all rush down the steps, into the yard for a view of the barn. They cluster together. The farmer says, "I don't see any smoke."

I follow the family down and stand still behind the boy, drinking his shadow, and it has all the things inside I hunt. I don't make a move to touch him on his arm fat with muscle, the skin browned from field work, or poke a finger through the hole torn in his shirt by the armpit and tickle. Patience is the quality most lacking in people of my group, and impulses must be recognized and arrested and considered before taking action, or else the flicker of a bad idea unchallenged can instantly make you swing a sharp instrument of hurt into the area of someone you had ought to love but can't for a second. I have learned exactly how patience looks when standing in public view and I strike that look in the farmer's yard.

Sleepy stares at the barn, tilting his head side to side as if confused by what he sees and wanting different angles, then says, "Oh, maybe you're right—it *ain't burnin'*, is it." He climbs into the truck, waves a small wave, fires the motor. I make those dots jump apart and back to-gether fast the way I walk swinging to the truck and hop into the seat. Sleepy eases us away on the lane real slow. I don't even need to look at the boy to know everything in his chest and how I'll collect him when the right movie shows. After we hit the paved road and go faster, Sleepy starts to whistle, not that well, a song I recognize before long, though, one of the ancient tunes we've all felt, but I couldn't put any name to it.

Returning the River

My brother left no footprints as he fled. There'd been three nights of freeze, and the mud had stiffened until the sloped field lay as hard as any slant road. Morning light met rime on the furrows and laid a shine between rows of cornstalks cut to winter spikes, and my brother, Harky, a mutinous man with a fog patch of gray hair drifting to the small of his back and black-booted feet, crushed the faded stalks aside as he came to them, and only these broken spikes marked his passing. His strides were long but curiosity curled his path, spun it about in small pondering circles as he glanced behind, followed by abrupt, total shifts in forward direction. The mud was unblemished but for the debris of cornstalks, and some of the pale dried shucks were spotted by kerosene drippings. Harky still carried the fuming torch he'd made of a baseball bat and a wadded sheet, the torch he'd used to set the neighbor's house afire, to make amends, to show his love, and flammable droplets fell beside him partway across the field.

Our father chased my brother. He chased him down the road from the burning house, into the field, wearing a white bathrobe and loose slippers. With each step he fell farther behind as his old sick feet skittered over uneven furrows and tripped. The nosepiece from his oxygen tube was yet pinched to his face, and a length of tube waved about while the robe flapped open. He fell repeatedly and stalks stabbed his skin broken at the ankles and hips. He stood up from the field six times, or only five, then again tripped over a furrow, collapsed to the frost, and lay there, face to the mud, withered fingers clenching at stalks, robe flung wide.

Smoke and shouts drifted from the neighbor's house.

Father's breathing could be heard beyond the fence line, up the road, the hoarse snatching after breath, rattling inhalations. He was raw beneath the robe, his skin ashen and his blood thinned by medications. The broken spots on his ankles and hips quickly turned blue and leaky. He held on to the oxygen tube with one hand, holding it still and inhaling, as if there might be a trapped bubble of pure oxygen his lungs could burst and pull through in shreds. Fogged eyeglasses hung from a cord around his neck, and his glum white private hair and forlorn flopping parts were open to the cold. He lay there weak as a babe, but a babe who'd already snuck a drink this morning, scotch, and chased it with a forbidden cigarette.

Across the mud and downslope he spotted Harky and his fog of hair scuttling from the field at the far end, plunging over the wire fence and into the thicket. Six foot two of man, with a jostling cloud riding his back and a blackened baseball bat in one hand.

Father rose to his knees, gasping, then stood and wobbled his way back to the road, legs too limber for firm strides, blood from his broken spots making lazy trails down his skin. Our father, the joking drunk who was so bitter when sober, shuffled past the edge of the fallow field, toward the big hunkered old house of glowering white that had been the home of our mother's family for three generations before recent inheritance delivered it down to us Dewlins. Mother waited near the door, pacing between the four-sided pillars on the veranda where she'd played jacks as a girl, hopscotch, her eyes glistening and rounded with anger. Her hair was a carefully selected chestnut hue, girlishly long and casually brushed, and she wore a winter coat belted over her bed clothes. She watched our father limp to the house and did not reach out to help him until he climbed the steps. They both paused on the veranda and looked across the road, toward the flames dancing on the shiny new log cottage of the only close neighbor, a man named Gordon Mather

Adams, a retired schoolteacher of some sort, a man I'd never spoken to, busy beside his eastern wall with a yellow garden hose and a panicked air, the excess water running from the flames down the slope of winter grass toward the river behind his house.

They stared for a few minutes, then she said, "I should've called in the fire, but…"

Father opened the door, crossed the threshold, and stepped onto the rug. He was bleeding from blue places, bleeding down his ankles, over that knob of bone, onto the large and intricate heirloom rug mother's people had always spread just inside the door, drop after drop.

Harky had waited for the holidays to fashion a torch and commit his spectacular act of penance, waited for me to be in the house, on the scene, his witness. Over the fence he'd gone, that fog bouncing about his head, into the forest, and I did not chase hard, did not even hurry, but let him spend his energy fleeing for a while. The trees stood towering gray and numb over us both, shorn of green uplift, the bark bared to the heavy sky and chapping wind. I suspect some stark limbs attempted to point Harky toward escape, others to wag in admonishment, blaming him for palming his pills and drinking whisky again. He hopped onto rocks in the creek to cross the stream, missed only one, and pushed up the slope with his left boot splashed and a sock growing soggy, choosing not to realize how the near future would treat a wet sock on a freezing day. The limb he'd trust most gestured this way, onto the animal path that curled around the hill in a spiral rising to the crest. He knocked aside branches and winter brambles with the baseball bat, and his feet crunched across wastes of leaves and twigs.

Harky is running toward places that aren't there anymore. That limb aimed him in the direction of the vanished cabin our mother's family first squatted in after they'd followed game trails west from Kentucky to claim these acres. He knows the general whereabouts of the old hearthstone, but the four walls have fallen and become mulch, and the yard is grown over with woods, blended again with the forest. One tree, many trees, where did the cabin sit? The rocks of the chimney were taken down and carted to the next house the Humphrieses built—high, wide, and white, across the creek on richer ground. In spring warmth the original spot might be found by looking for brighter colors paraded amidst the bland grasses: irises, daffodils, columbine. Great-great-great-grandma with the first name blown from her headstone and lost for good was quick to put down flowers near the house, dollops of cultivation in the yard that meant we live here now, inside this wilderness, and those common perennials are the only remains of a family place abandoned.

In his sick final years Grandpa Humphries sold the pasture, the cornfields, the wooded hillocks and ridges, sold every acre but the two that made a lawn for the house. He'd feared he might live closer to forever than predicted and need those dollars to find rest in his mind. Harky kneels to our old ground and rubs his hands through the sodden leaves, pushing them aside, making one tiny clearing after another, looking for nubs, withered blades of green. His breath puffs signals that don't last. Dead grasses fly to his clothes and cling. Dirt buries beneath his fingernails. He's in high spirits for a man who knows that his parole will be revoked in about an hour, maybe two. There's a pint bottle in his jacket and he stands up for a ruminative chug, but it is empty except for a few drops that are slow reaching his lips. He looks around the ground, studies trees he might know from years before, but doesn't spot any old acquaintances, and moves on farther behind the hill. He just can't find Granny-what's-her-name's flowers during this cold season.

The path is steep and vague in spots, barely there, with a few crashed trees to be crawled across or jumped. Running these woods Harky is feeling redeemed in his bones, raised in his heart, a much better son now than he was before dawn. We'd often hunted this land together when down from the city during holidays, boys afield in joyous pursuit of the small and wild, sharing our single-shot Sears twenty-two, avoiding the tensions in the house for hours at a stretch. I'd pop squirrels from limbs, since they have more taste, but Harky favored rabbits because they were easier to skin. When snow had fallen over the meadows, he'd delight in tracking bunnies at dawn, stealthily following paw prints as they made circles easy to follow, then track the same paw prints around again, and again, never caring that if he just waited where he started the rabbits would circle back within range and offer themselves to his aim: "But tracking is the fun part!" The air on the ridge is cold and smacks of fire, and when I make the turn at the crest, the pinnacle suddenly revealed, Harky is sitting calmly on a large slab rock watching the flames in the valley. That fog of hair drapes past where his ass meets the slab and dangles. The bat stood upright between his legs, black end down.

He said, "Think he'll be happy now?"

"You didn't get far."

"I knew they'd send you—bring any whisky?"

The seal hadn't been cracked on the bottle I handed to him. He busted the whisky open and swallowed a big peaty breakfast, released a deep groan of appreciation, and dropped the cap into his pocket. I sat on the slab beside him. The mess of smoke below had grown. Deputies were standing in the road, and the volunteer fire department was arriving in pickups, little cars, dusty vans, and the one official fire truck they kept ready at Bing Plimmer's gas station.

"Is that house fully involved?"

Two men in waders dragged a hose toward the river, hunching away from the jumping heat. The deputies in the street seemed excited and were gathering around our mother, but she's an old hand at this and stands still, with her arms folded, and listens without argument. Harky's parole would be violated any minute now.

"I think that's what they call it."

"Then it might still burn down flat."

"The man'll only build it back again with insurance money. Maybe bigger."

"But not in time."

"He might live longer than you think."

"No. He'll die seein' the river where it's supposed to be again."

Those distant faces so tiny in the valley turned together and stared roughly in our direction. Harky laughed at them, pointed with his fist, and thumped the ball bat to ground. The fire seemed to be winning. Gordon Mather Adams looked to be weeping. Mother had been angry since the foundation was poured, the first nail driven, and clapped her hands with gusto as the hot ruin spread. A sheriff's car began to roll down the sloped road alongside the field. I swatted my brother on the knee and stood.

"Let's get deeper into the woods," I said. "Make it harder for them."

"You want to run with me?"

He passed the bottle, and I said, "You'll be gone a long time this time, Harky."

"Ahh, I have friends in the slams, baby brother, so don't worry." He raised from the slab and shuffled his feet, then sat again and pulled the boot and sock from his wet foot. The skin looked red. He wrung the sock until droplets fell, then pulled it on damp and laced up. He stood, happy with himself and smiling at the smoke in the sky, the voices all excited in the distance. "I could use a new little TV. With better color. And headphones."

Two walls were coming down. They folded inward and smashed across smoldering furniture and seared appliances, sparks bursting and riding the heat. The flames were renewed by the falling and frolicked. One more wall to fall and father could die upstairs with the river back in his eyes.

I gave Harky the bottle, wiped my lips dry. "Today's got to be worth a party."

The sheriff's car had stopped on the road and the deputy stood in the opened door talking into the radio, calling for help. He was studying the woods, looking for paths he might follow to give chase, but we remembered them all from before we were born and walked on laughing, down the spiraled path to low ground and away through a rough patch of scrub, into a small stand of pine trees and the knowing shadow they laid over us, our history, our trespassing boots.

WINTER'S BONE

Daniel Woodrell

'A marvellous writer' Roddy Doyle

'Deep in the mountains of Missouri, you can get beaten up for asking the wrong questions, everyone knows how to fire a gun, and most families are cooking up crank on the back porch. A teenage girl takes on more than she bargains for when she sets out to find her missing father ... Brutal, violent and completely gripping.'
Independent on Sunday

'Woodrell throws down sentences that will leave you amazed'
Charles Frazier

'Reading this will make you feel like you walk on very, very thin ice, and know that chaos is very, very close. Such knowledge has many consequences, one of them is exhilaration.'
Niall Griffiths, *Observer*

'It brings us all the satisfactions of crime thriller and mystery ... The beauty lies in the loveable and wholly believable character of Ree'
Stevie Davies, *Guardian*

'A suspicion grows that you are reading the sort of book D.B.C Pierre's Vernon God Little might have been, had it been five times as keenly observed and deeply felt'
Tom Cox, *The Times*

'He belongs in the forefront of American fiction.'
John Williams, *Independent*

S

SCEPTRE